'I came to take you back.'

'I'm sorry you had a wasted journey, Franco,' she said firmly, 'but I'm very busy for the next few days—'

'I told you I'd cleared it with your employer—'

'But you neglected to clear it with me. I do have some feelings.'

Franco gave Joanne a strange look, and she guessed he was remembering how she'd betrayed herself in his arms.

'I don't ask for myself,' he said at last, 'but for my son. You won Nico's heart. Do I have to tell you how precious a gift that is? Did you delight him only to amuse yourself, and to throw him aside when it suits you?'

'Of course not. That's a wicked thing to say.'

'Then come back with me now. It will mean the world to him—and to me.'

Lucy Gordon cut her writing teeth on magazine journalism, interviewing many of the world's most interesting men, including Warren Beatty, Richard Chamberlain, Roger Moore, Sir Alec Guinness and Sir John Gielgud. She also camped out with lions in Africa, and had many other unusual experiences which have often provided the background for her books. She is married to a Venetian, whom she met while on holiday in Venice. They got engaged within two days, and have now been married for twenty-five years. They live in the Midlands, with their three dogs.

Recent titles by the same author:

THE DIAMOND DAD
BE MY GIRL!

FARELLI'S WIFE

BY
LUCY GORDON

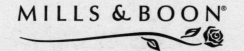

This book is dedicated to Flump,
a loyal friend and beautiful dog,
whose loss inspired the poem in the last chapter.

First published in Great Britain 1998
Harlequin Mills & Boon Limited,
Eton House, 18-24 Paradise Road, Richmond, Surrey TW9 1SR

© Lucy Gordon 1999

ISBN 0 263 81734 2

Set in Times Roman 10½ on 12 pt.
02-9907-48207 C1

Printed and bound in Norway
by Litografia Rosés, S.A., Barcelona

PROLOGUE

THE headstone stood in the shadow of trees. A small stream rippled softly past, and flowers crept up to the foot of the white marble. The engraving said simply that here lay Rosemary Farelli, beloved wife of Franco Farelli, and mother of Nico. The inscription showed that she had died exactly a year ago, aged thirty-two, and with her, her unborn child.

There were other headstones in the Farelli burial plot, but only this one had a path worn right up to it, as though someone was drawn back here time and again, someone who had yet to come to terms with the heartbreaking finality of that stone.

Three figures appeared through the little wood that surrounded the plot. The first was a middle-aged woman with a grim expression and upright carriage. Behind her came a man in his thirties, whose dark eyes held a terrible bleakness. One hand rested lightly on the shoulder of the little boy walking beside him, his hands full of wild flowers.

The woman approached the grave and stood regarding it for a moment. Her face was hard and expressionless. A stranger, coming upon the group, might have wondered if she'd felt any affection for the dead woman. At last she stood aside and the man stepped forward.

'Let me take Nico home,' she said. 'This is no place for a child.'

5

The man's face was dark. 'He is Rosemary's son. This is his right—and his mother's.'

'Franco, she's dead.'

'Not here.' He touched his breast and spoke softly. 'Not ever.' He looked down at the child. 'Are you ready, *piccino?*'

The little boy, as fair as his father was dark, looked up and nodded. He laid the flowers at the foot of the grave. 'These are for you, Mama,' he said.

When he stepped back his father's hand rested again on his shoulder.

'Well done,' he said quietly to his son. 'I'm proud of you. Now go home with your grandmama.'

'Can't I stay with you, Papa?'

Franco Farelli's face was gentle. 'Not now. I must be alone with your mother.'

He stood quite still until they had gone. Not until their footsteps faded into silence did he move towards the gravestone and kneel before it, whispering.

'I brought our son to you, *mi amore*. See how he has grown, how strong and beautiful he is. Soon he will be seven years old. He hasn't forgotten you. Every day we talk together about "Mama". I'm raising him as you wished, to remember that he is English as well as Italian. He speaks his mother's tongue as well as his father's.'

His eyes darkened with pain. 'He looks more like you every day. How can I bear that? This morning he turned to me with the smile that was yours, and it was as though you were there. But the next moment you died again, and my heart broke.

'It is one year to the day since you died, and still the world is dark for me. When you left you took joy with you. I try to be a good father to our child, but my heart is with you, and my life is a desert.'

He reached out a hand to touch the unyielding marble. 'Are you there, my beloved? Where have you gone? Why can I not find you?'

Suddenly his control broke. His fingers grasped the marble convulsively, his eyes closed and a cry of terrible anguish broke from him.

'Come back to me! I can bear it no longer. *For God's sake, come back to me!*'

CHAPTER ONE

IF JOANNE concentrated hard she could bring the brush down to the exact point, and turn it at the very last minute. It took great precision, but she'd rehearsed the movement often, and now she could do it right, every time.

The result was perfect, just as the whole picture was perfect—a perfect copy. The original was a little masterpiece. Beside it stood her own version, identical in every brush stroke. Except that she could only trudge slowly where genius had shown the way.

The dazzling afternoon sunlight streaming through the windows of the Villa Antonini showed Joanne how well she'd performed her allotted task, and how mediocre that task was.

'Is it finished?' Signor Vito Antonini had crept into the room and come to stand beside her. He was a tubby man in late middle age who'd made a huge fortune in engineering and was now enjoying spending it. He showered gifts on his plain little wife, whom he adored, and had bought her this luxurious villa on the outskirts of Turin.

Then he'd purchased some great paintings to adorn it. But because they were valuable the insurers had insisted that they should all be locked away in the bank, which wasn't what he'd wanted at all. So he'd sent for Joanne Merton, who, at only twenty-seven, had a fast-rising reputation as a copyist, specializing in Italian paintings.

'Your copies are so perfect that nobody will know the difference, *signorina*,' he said now, gleefully.

'I'm glad you're satisfied with my work,' Joanne said, with a smile. She liked the little man and his wife, who'd welcomed her into their home and treated her like an honoured guest.

'Do you think,' he asked wistfully, 'that we could put your pictures in the bank vaults and keep the originals on my walls?'

'No,' she said hastily. 'Vito, I'm a copyist, not a forger. You know the condition of my work is that it's never passed off as the original.'

Vito sighed, for he was a risk-taker, but just then his wife came into the room and Joanne appealed to her.

'*Cretino*,' she admonished her husband briskly. 'You want this nice girl to go to gaol? Forget this silly idea and come and eat.'

'More food?' Joanne protested, laughing. 'Are you trying to make me fat, Maria?'

'I'm trying to stop you fading away,' Maria said. 'No girl should be as thin as you are.'

Joanne wasn't really thin, but elegantly slim. She was fighting to stay that way, but Maria made it hard.

The table was groaning under the fruit of her labours: garlic bread and tomatoes, black olive pâté and fish soup, followed by rice and peas.

Despite her concern for her figure, Joanne couldn't resist this mouth-watering repast. She'd loved Piedmont cooking since she was eighteen and had won a scholarship to study art in Italy. She'd been blissfully happy, tucking into the rich, spicy meals, or wandering through Turin, drunk on great paintings, dreaming that one day she would contribute to their number. And

she'd fallen wildly, passionately in love with Franco
Farelli.

She'd met him through his sister, Renata, an art student in the same class. They'd become good friends,
and Renata had taken her home to meet her family,
wine growers with huge vineyards just north of the
little medieval town of Asti. Joanne had fallen in love
with Isola Magia, the Farelli home, and been instantly
at ease with the whole family: Giorgio, the big, boom-
ing papa who laughed a lot, and drank a lot and bawled
a lot; Sophia, his wife, a sharp-faced, sharp-tempered
woman who'd greeted Joanne with restraint, but made
her welcome.

But from the moment she'd met Franco she'd known
she'd come home in a totally different way. He'd been
twenty-four, tall and long-boned, with a proud carriage
that set him apart from other men. His height came
from his father, a northern Italian. But his mother
hailed from Naples down in the south, and from her he
derived his swarthy looks, dark chocolate eyes and
blue-black hair.

In other ways, too, he was an amalgam of north and
south. He had Giorgio's easygoing charm, but also
Sophia's volcanic temper and quick, killing rages.
Joanne had seen that rage only once, when he'd found
a young man viciously tormenting a dog. He'd knocked
the lout down with one blow, and for a moment his
eyes had contained murder.

He'd taken the dog home and tended it as gently as
a woman, eagerly assisted by Renata and Joanne. That
night the dog's owner had returned with his two brothers, drunk and belligerent, demanding the return of
their 'property'. Joanne would never forget what had
happened next.

Calmly Franco had taken out a wicked-looking sti-
letto, thrust the blade through some paper money and
held it out to them.

'This will pay for the dog,' he'd said coldly. 'Take
it and never trouble me again.'

But the brothers hadn't touched the money.
Something they'd seen in Franco's eyes had sent them
fleeing out into the night, yammering with fear, never
to return. The dog had been named Ruffo, and become
his inseparable companion.

But such incidents had been rare. Franco had been
more concerned with enjoying himself than fighting.
For him there had always been a joke to be relished, a
song to be sung, a girl to be wooed, and perhaps more
than wooed, if she was willing. When he'd smiled his
white teeth had gleamed against his tanned skin, and
he'd seemed like a young god of the earth.

Until then Joanne hadn't believed in love at first
sight, but she'd known at once that she belonged to
Franco, body and soul. Just looking at him had been
able to make her flesh grow warmer, even in that fierce
Italian heat. His smile had made her feel she were melt-
ing, and she would gladly have melted if, by doing so,
she could have become a part of him.

His smile. She could see it now, slow and teasing,
as though the world were his and he was wondering
whom to share it with. And she knew, by instinct, what
kind of a world it was: one of desire and satiation, of
sinking his strong teeth into life's delights while the
pleasure overflowed, of heated taking and giving, living
by the rhythms of the earth that received the seed so
that there should be growing, reaping and growing
again. She had known all this the first time she'd seen
him, striding into the flagstoned kitchen and standing

near the door, his black hair turned to blue by a shaft
of light, calling, 'Hey, Mama—' in a ringing voice.

How could anyone resist that voice? It was rich with
all the passion in the world, as though he'd made love
to every woman he'd met. And Joanne, the girl from
a cool, rainy country, had known in a blinding instant
that he was her destiny.

Sadly, she had no illusions that she was his destiny.
The estate was filled with lush virgins and ripe young
matrons who sighed for him. She knew, because
Renata had confided, between giggles, that Franco took
his pleasures freely, wherever they might be found, to
the outrage of his mother and the secret envy of his
father.

But he had never even flirted with Joanne, treating
her just as he had his sister, teasing her amiably before
passing on his way, his exuberant laughter floating behind him. And her heart had been ready to burst with
joy at his presence and despair at his indifference.

'I couldn't eat another thing,' Joanne declared, regarding her clean plate.

'But you must have some cream cheese and rum
pudding,' Maria said. 'You're working her too hard,'
she scolded her husband.

'It's not my fault,' he protested. 'I show her the pictures and say, ''Work as you like,'' and in a week she
has finished the copy of the Carracci Madonna.'

'Because she works too much,' Maria insisted, slap-
ping cream cheese on Joanne's plate. 'How many are
still to do?'

'Four,' Joanne said. 'Two more by Carracci, one
Giotto and one Veronese. I'm saving the Veronese until
last because it's so large.'

'I can't believe that an English girl understands Italian paintings so well,' Vito mused. 'At the start I had the names of several Italians who do this work, but everyone said to me, "No, you must go to Signorina Merton, who is English, but has an Italian soul."'

'I studied in Italy for a year,' Joanne reminded him.

'Only for a year? One would think you had lived here all your life. That must have been a wonderful year, for I think Italy entered deep into your heart.'

'Yes,' Joanne said slowly. 'It did…'

Renata began inviting her every weekend and Joanne lived for these visits. Franco was always there because the vineyard was his life and he'd learned its management early. Despite his youth he was already taking the reins from his papa's hands, and running the place better than Giorgio ever had.

Once Joanne managed to catch him among the vines when he was alone. He was feeling one bunch after another, his long, strong fingers squeezing them as tenderly as a lover. She smiled up at him. She was five feet nine inches, and Franco was one of the few men tall enough to make her look up.

'I came out for some fresh air,' she said, trying to sound casual.

'You chose the best time,' he told her with his easy smile that made her feel as if the world had lit up around her. 'I love it out here at evening when the air is soft and kind.'

He finished with an eyebrow raised in quizzical enquiry, for he'd spoken in Italian, a language she was still learning.

'Morbida e gentile,' she repeated, savouring the

words. 'Soft and kind. But it isn't really that sort of country, is it?'

'It can be. Italy has its violent moods, but it can be sweet and tender.'

How deep and resonant his voice was. It seemed to vibrate through her, turning her bones to water. She sought something to say that would sound poised.

'It's a beautiful sunset,' she managed at last. 'I'd love to paint it.'

'Are you going to be a great artist, *piccina?*' he asked teasingly.

She wished he wouldn't call her *piccina*. It meant 'little girl' and was used in speaking to children. Yet it was also a term of affection and she treasured it as a crumb from his table.

'I think so,' she said, as if considering the matter seriously. 'But I'm still trying to find my own style.'

She hadn't yet learned that she had no individual style, only a gift for imitation.

Without answering he pulled down a small bunch of grapes and crushed a few against his mouth. The purple juice spilled out luxuriantly down his chin, like the wine of life, she thought. Eagerly she held out her hands and he pulled off a spray of the grapes and offered them to her. She imitated his movement, pressing the fruit against her mouth, then gagged at the taste.

'They're sour,' she protested indignantly.

'Sharp,' he corrected. 'The sun hasn't ripened them yet. It'll happen in its own good time, as everything does.'

'But how can you eat them when they taste like this?'

'Sharp or sweet, they are as they are. They're still

the finest fruit in all Italy.' It was a simple statement, unblushing in its arrogance.

'There are other places with fine grapes,' she said, nettled at his assurance. 'What about the Po valley, or the Romagna?'

He didn't even dignify this with an answer, merely lifted his shoulders in a slight shrug, as if other vineyards weren't worth considering.

'What a pity you won't be here to taste them when they're ripe,' he said. 'That won't be until August, and you'll have returned to England.'

His words brought home to her how near their parting was. Her time in Italy was almost over, and then she wouldn't see him again. He was the love of her life but he didn't know, would never know.

She was desperate for something that would make him notice her, but while she was racking her brains she saw a movement among the vines. It was Virginia, a voluptuous and poorly named young woman who'd occupied a lot of Franco's attention recently.

Franco had seen her and turned laughing eyes on Joanne, not in the least embarrassed. 'And now you must go, *piccina*, for I have matters to attend to.'

Crushing disappointment made her adopt a haughty tone. 'I'm sorry if I'm in the way.'

'You are,' he said shamelessly. 'Terribly in the way. Run along now, like a good girl.'

She bit her lip at being treated like a child, and turned away with as much dignity as she could muster. She didn't look back, but she couldn't help hearing the girl's soft, provocative laughter.

She lay awake that night, listening for Franco. He didn't return until three in the morning. She heard him humming softly as he passed her door, and then she buried her head under the pillow and wept.

The time began to rush past and the end of her final term grew inexorably nearer. Joanne received a letter from her cousin Rosemary who would be taking a vacation in Italy at that time. She wrote:

> I thought I'd come to Turin just before you finish, and we can travel home together.

Joanne and Rosemary had grown up together, and most people, seeing them side by side, had thought that they were sisters. They'd actually lived as sisters after Joanne's parents had died and Rosemary had urged her widowed mother to take the girl in.

She'd been twelve then, and Joanne six. When Rosemary's mother had died six years later Rosemary had assumed the role of mother. Joanne had adored the cousin who'd given her a home and security, and all the love in her big, generous heart.

As Joanne had grown up they'd become more alike. They had both been unusually tall women, with baby blonde hair, deep blue eyes and peach colouring. Their features had been cast from the same mould, but Rosemary's had been fine and delicate, whereas Joanne's had still been blurred by youth and teenage chubbiness.

But the real difference, the one that had always tormented Joanne, had lain in Rosemary's poise and charm. She had been supremely confident of her own beauty and she'd moved through life dazzling everyone she met, winning hearts easily.

Joanne had been awed by the ease with which her

cousin had claimed life as her own. She'd wanted to be like her. She'd wanted to *be* her, and it had been frustrating to have been trapped in her own, ordinary self, so like Rosemary, and yet so cruelly unlike her in all that mattered.

At other times she'd wanted to be as different from Rosemary as possible, to escape her shadow and be herself. When people had said, 'You're going to be as pretty as Rosemary one day,' she'd known they'd meant to be kind, but the words had made her grind her teeth.

She could remember, as if it were yesterday, the night of the party, given by a fellow student. Joanne and Renata had been going together, with Franco escorting them, but at the last minute Renata had sprained her ankle and dropped out. Joanne had been in ecstasies at having Franco all to herself.

She'd bought a new dress and spent hours putting up her hair and perfecting her make-up. Surely that night he would notice her, even perhaps ask her to stay in Italy? Her heart had been singing as she'd gone down to where he'd been waiting outside on the terrace.

He'd been dressed for the evening. She'd never seen him formally attired before, but then she'd been struck afresh by how handsome he'd been with his snowy shirt against his swarthy skin. He'd looked up and smiled, raising his eyebrows in appreciation of her enhanced appearance.

'So, *piccina,* you've decided to take the world by storm tonight?' he teased.

'I just dressed up a little,' she said, trying to be casual, but with a horrible suspicion that she sounded as gauche as she felt.

'You'll break all their hearts,' he promised her.

'Oh, I don't know about *all* their hearts,' she said with a shrug.

'Just the one you want, eh?'

Could he have suspected? she wondered with sudden excitement. Was this his way of saying that he'd finally noticed her?

'Maybe I haven't decided which one I want,' she said archly, looking up at him.

He chuckled, and the sound filled her with happy expectation. 'Perhaps I should help you decide,' he said, and reached out to take gentle hold of her chin.

At last! The thing she'd prayed for, wept for, longed for, was happening. He was going to kiss her. As he lifted her chin and his mouth hovered above hers she was on the verge of heaven. She raised her hands, tentatively touching his arms.

And then it was all snatched away. There was a step in the passage, and a woman's voice floated out to them.

'I'm sorry to arrive without warning—'

Franco stopped, his mouth an inch above hers, raising his head, alerted by the voice. Joanne felt the shock that went through his body. He'd heard only Rosemary's voice, but already some special timbre in it seemed to tell him what was about to happen. He stepped away from Joanne, towards the door.

The next moment Rosemary appeared. Joanne, watching with jealous eyes that saw every detail, knew that all the breath had gone out of him, so that he stood like a man poised between two lives. Later she realized that this was literally true. Franco had seen his fate walk through the door, with long blonde hair and a

dazzling smile. And he'd instantly recognized that this
was what she was. He was no longer the same man.

Dazed, hardly able to believe what had happened,
Joanne turned her eyes to see Rosemary staring at
Franco with the same look that he was giving her. It
was all over in a flash, and there was nothing to be
done about it.

There were hasty introductions. Rosemary greeted
everyone and threw her arms about Joanne, while
somehow never taking her eyes off Franco. He was like
a man in a dream. It was his idea that Rosemary come
to the party with them. Joanne wanted to cry out at
having come so close to her desire, but what would be
the use of that? Even she could see that what was happening had always been meant.

At the party Franco monopolized Rosemary, dancing
almost every dance with her, plying her with food and
wine. His good manners made him attend to Joanne's
comfort, watching to make sure that she wasn't a wallflower. There was no danger of that since she was pop-
ular. She danced every dance, determined not to show
that her heart was breaking, and when Franco saw that
she had a supply of partners he forgot her and spent
every moment with Rosemary.

Many times she wondered what would have happened if Rosemary had seen her in Franco's arms.
Would she have taken him, knowing how Joanne loved
him? But the question was pointless. Franco pursued
Rosemary fiercely through the evening that followed
and every day afterwards until he made her his own.
He was like a man driven by demons until he came to
the safe haven of his love.

It was still painful to recall how she slipped away
from the dance and stumbled across them in each

other's arms, in the darkness. She backed away, but not before she heard Franco murmuring, '*Mi amore*— I will love you until I die,' and saw him kiss her passionately. It was so different from the teasing kiss he'd almost bestowed on herself, and she fled, weeping frantically.

Apart from herself, the only person not pleased by the wedding was Sophia. Joanne overheard the family scene in which Sophia begged Franco to marry a local girl, and not 'this stranger, who knows nothing of our ways'. Franco refused to quarrel with his mother, but he insisted on his right to marry the woman of his choice. He also demanded, quietly but firmly, that his bride should be treated with respect. Joanne was struck by the change in him. Already the easygoing lad who'd once let his mother's tirades wash over him was turning into a man of serious purpose. Sophia evidently felt it too, for she burst into angry tears.

'Poor Mama,' Renata observed. 'Franco's always been her favourite, and now she's jealous because he loves Rosemary best.'

The whole neighbourhood was invited to their wedding. Joanne longed not to be there, but Rosemary asked her and Renata to be her bridesmaids. Joanne was afraid that if she refused everyone would guess why.

When the day came she put on her pink satin dress, smiled despite her heartbreak, and walked behind Rosemary as she went down the aisle to become Franco's wife. Joanne saw the look on his face as he watched his bride's approach. It was a look of total, blind adoration, and it tore the heart out of her.

A year later she pleaded work as an excuse not to attend the baptism of their son, Nico. Rosemary wrote to her affectionately, saying how sorry she was not to see her again, and enclosing some christening cake and photographs. Joanne studied them jealously, noting how the same look was still on Franco's face when he looked at his wife. Even in the flat photographs it blazed out, the gaze of a supremely happy man whose marriage had brought him love and fulfilment. She hid the pictures away.

After that there were more pictures, showing Nico growing fast out of babyhood, becoming an eager toddler learning to walk, held safe by his father's hands. Franco's face grew a little older, less boyish. And always it bore the same look, that of a man who'd found all he wanted in life.

Rosemary stayed in touch through occasional telephone calls, and long letters, with photographs enclosed. Joanne knew everything that happened on the Farelli farm, almost as well as if she'd been there. Renata married an art dealer and went to live in Milan. Franco's father died. Two years later his mother visited her sister in Naples, where she met a widower with two children and married him. Franco, Rosemary and baby Nico were left alone on the farm: alone, that was, except for a woman who helped with the housework, and the dozens of vineyard workers who wandered in and out of the house.

Rosemary often repeated her loving invitations. She wrote:

It seems so long since we saw you. You shouldn't be a stranger, darling, especially after we were so close once.

Joanne would write back, excusing herself on the grounds of work, for her skill in copying paintings to

the last brush stroke had made her a successful career.
But she never gave the true reason, which was that she
didn't trust herself to look at Rosemary's husband
without loving him. And that was forbidden, not only
because he cared nothing for her, but because Joanne
also loved Rosemary.

She had no other close family, and the cousin who
was also sister and mother was dearer to her than anyone on earth, except Franco. She owed Rosemary more
than she could repay, and her fierce sense of loyalty
made her keep her distance.

She was lonely, and sometimes the temptation to pay
a visit was overwhelming. Surely it could do no harm
to meet little Nico, enjoy the farm life for a while, and
be enveloped in the warmth and love that Rosemary
seemed to carry with her at all times?

But then Rosemary would write, innocently ending
the letter, 'Franco sends his love'. And the words still
hurt, warning her that the visit must never be made.

She'd been eighteen when she'd fallen in love with
him, and it should have been one of those passing teenage infatuations, so common at that age. Her misfor-
tune was that it wasn't. Instead of getting over Franco
she'd gone on cherishing his image with a despairing
persistence that warned her never to risk seeing him.

To outward appearances Joanne was a successful
woman, with a string of admirers. The chubbiness of
her early years had gone, leaving her figure slender and
her face delicate. There were always men eager to follow her beauty and a certain indefinable something in
her air. She let them wine and dine her and some of
them, blind to the remote signals she sent out without
knowing it, deceived themselves that they were making

progress. When they realized their mistake they called
her heartless, and to a point it was true. She had no
heart for them. Her heart had been stolen long ago by
a man who didn't want it.

Then Rosemary returned to England for a visit,
bringing her five-year-old son. They stayed with
Joanne for a week, and some of their old closeness was
restored. They talked for hours into the night. Joanne
was enchanted by the little boy. He looked English, but
he had the open-heartedness of his Italian father, and
would snuggle on her lap as happily as on his mother's.

Rosemary watched the two of them fondly, while she
talked of her life in Italy with the husband she adored.
The only flaw was Sophia's continuing hostility.

'I don't know what I'd have done if she hadn't re-
married,' she confessed. 'She hates me.'

'But she was always nagging Franco to get married,'
Joanne recalled.

'Yes, but she wanted to choose his wife. She'd have
picked a local girl who wouldn't have competed with
her for his heart, and given him lots and lots of children. Franco really wants them. Sophia never lets me
forget that I've only managed to give him one.

'I've tried and tried to make her my friend, but it's
useless. She hates me because Franco loves me so
much, and I couldn't change that—even if I wanted
to.'

Her words made Joanne recall how Sophia's manner
to herself had altered without warning. She'd been
friendly enough, in her sharp manner, until one day
she'd caught Joanne regarding Franco with yearning in
her eyes. After that she'd grown cool, as though nobody but herself was allowed to love him.

Rosemary's face was radiant as she talked of her

husband. 'I never knew such happiness could exist,' she said in a voice full of wonder. 'Oh, darling, if only it could happen for you too.'

'I'm a career woman,' Joanne protested, hiding her face against Nico's hair lest it reveal some forbidden consciousness. 'I'll probably never marry.'

She was the first to learn Rosemary's thrilling secret.

'I haven't even told Franco yet, because I don't want to raise false hopes,' she admitted. 'But he wants another child so badly, and I want to give him one.'

A week after her return to Italy she telephoned to say she was certain at last, and Franco was over the moon.

But the child was never born. In the fifth month of her pregnancy Rosemary collapsed with a heart attack, and died.

Joanne was in Australia at the time, working against a deadline. It would have been impractical to go to Italy for the funeral, but the truth was she was glad of the excuse to stay away. Her love for Rosemary's husband tormented her with guilt now that Rosemary was dead.

The year that followed was the most miserable of her life. Despite their long parting, Rosemary had stayed in touch so determinedly that she had remained a vital part of her life. Joanne only truly understood that now that she was gone, and the empty space yawned.

She had several requests to work in Italy, but she turned them all down on one pretext or another. Then a debilitating bout of flu left her too weak to work for some time, and her bank balance grew dangerously low. When the offer came from Vito Antonini she was glad of the chance to make some money.

He lived only sixty miles away from Franco. But she

could shut herself up to work, and never venture into the outside world. There was no need to see him if she didn't want to. So, despite her misgivings, she accepted the job and flew to Italy, telling herself that she was in no danger, and trying to believe it.

CHAPTER TWO

'WHY you never take the car?' Maria demanded one day. 'When you arrive I say, 'We don't need the second car. You use it.' But you never do. Is very unkind.'

'Don't be offended, Maria, please,' Joanne begged. 'It's just that I've been so busy.'

'Don't you have any friends from when you were here before?'

'Well—my cousin's family lives near Asti—'

'And you haven't visited?' Maria shrieked in horror, for like all Italians she was family-minded. 'You go now.'

Vito backed his wife up, and the two of them virtually ordered her out of the house.

'You stay away tonight,' Maria ordered. 'You won't have time to drive back.'

'I'll have plenty of time,' Joanne insisted. 'I'm only going for a couple of hours.'

They argued about this until the last minute, Maria demanding that she pack a bag, Joanne firmly refusing. She was going to make this visit as brief as possible, just to prove to herself that she could cope with meeting Franco. Then she would leave and never go back.

She was dressed for the country, in trousers and sweater. But both had come from one of Turin's most expensive shops, and she added a gold chain about her waist and dainty gold studs in her ears. She didn't realize that she was making a point, but the costly ele-

gance of her attire marked her out as a different person
from the gauche girl of eight years ago.

As soon as she got out onto the road and felt the
beauty of the day, and the sun streaming in through the
open window, Joanne was glad. She'd been shut up too
long with the smell of oil paint and turpentine, and she
needed to breathe fresh air.

She took the route through the little medieval town
of Asti. Already there were posters up advertising the
palio, the bareback race that was run every year around
the *piazza.* The jockeys were all local lads, and
Joanne's mind went back to the time Franco had taken
part.

She'd been nervous as she'd taken her place in the
stands with the family and almost every worker from
the Farelli vineyard. The *palio* was so fierce that mat-
tresses were fixed to the walls of all the surrounding
buildings to save the riders and horses who crashed into
them. Even so, injuries were common.

After the first lap it had been clear that the race was
between Franco and another rider.

'That's Leo,' Renata said excitedly. 'He and Franco
are good friends—except today.'

It was neck and neck on the last lap. Then Leo went
ahead. Franco made a desperate attempt to catch up.
The crowd's cheers turned to screams as the horses
collided and both riders were thrown. Miraculously the
following riders managed to jump over them, and neither man was hurt. But Joanne's heart was in her mouth
as they all hurried around to see Franco afterwards.

Sophia clung to him, almost suffocating him until
Giorgio gently prised her away. Leo hurled his whip
to the ground, complaining, 'I was winning. I had the
race in the palm of my hand. And he robbed me.'

Franco offered Leo his hand. Leo stared at it until everyone thought he would refuse to shake. At last he put out his own hand, saying through a forced smile, 'I'll get even with you next year, Farelli. See if I don't.'

But Franco had never competed again. By the next race he'd been married to Rosemary, looking forward to starting a family.

Joanne parked the car and spent an hour wandering the streets she'd once known so well. She decided she might as well have lunch here too, and enjoyed a leisurely pizza. She would have denied that she was putting off her meeting with Franco, but she didn't hurry.

But when she resumed the journey she was further delayed by a traffic jam. For two hours she fretted and fumed behind a trail of trucks, and it was late afternoon before she neared the Farelli vineyards. She parked the car off the road and got out to lean over a fence and survey the land. The vines were growing strongly and everywhere she looked she saw the brightness of summer. It reminded her of her year in Italy when she'd fallen in love with Franco.

What would he be like now? Her last picture of him had been taken eighteen months ago and showed him older, more serious, as befitted a man of responsibilities. Yet even then a mischievous devil still lurked in his eyes. But he must have changed again since the death of his beloved wife. Suddenly she was afraid to see him. He would be a stranger.

But she couldn't give up now. Courtesy demanded that she see Rosemary's widower and child before she left the district. She started up again and drove on to the turning that led to the house. At once memory began to play back. The dirt track was still the one she'd seen the day Renata had brought her here for the first time. There were the ruts left by the trucks that regularly arrived and departed.

The big, sprawling house too was the same, yellow ochre in the blazing sun, the dark green shutters pulled closed against the heat, the roof tiles rusty red. And everywhere there were geraniums, the brightly coloured flowers without which no Italian country home seemed complete. Geraniums around the doors, in window boxes, in hanging baskets: red, white, pink, purple, every petal glowing vividly in the brilliant light.

Chickens strutted pompously back and forth in the yard, uttering soft, contented clucks. The Farelli family was wealthy, but the house was that of a prosperous farmer, with homeliness prevailing over luxury. That was its charm.

Did nothing ever change here? There was the long table under the trees with the benches at either side. Above it stood the wooden trellis roof with flowers wreathing in and out and hanging down from it. How many times had she sat beneath those flowers, as if in paradise, listening to the family backchat over a meal? Paradise that might have been hers, that could never have been hers. Paradise lost.

The front door was open and she walked inside. Rosemary had made this place her own, but it still felt familiar. The few new pieces of furniture blended in with the warm red flagstones. The huge fireplace, where the family had warmed themselves by log fires, was unchanged. The old sofa had been re-covered, but was otherwise still the same, the largest one Joanne had ever seen.

The staircase led directly out of the main room. An old woman whom Joanne had never seen before came bustling downstairs, wiping her hands on her apron.

She was dressed in black, save for a coloured scarf covering her hair. She stopped very still when she saw Joanne.

'I'm sorry to come in uninvited,' Joanne said quickly. 'I'm not prying. My cousin was Signor Farelli's wife. Is he here?'

'He is with the vines on the south slope,' the woman said slowly. 'I will send for him.'

'No need. I know where it is. *Grazie.*'

In the poor light of the stairs she hadn't noticed the old woman's face grow pale at the sight of her. And she went out too quickly to hear her murmur, *'Maria vergine!'* or see her cross herself.

She remembered the way perfectly. She followed the path to the stream, stepping gingerly across the stones that punctuated the fast-running water. Once she'd pretended to lose her nerve in the middle of those stones so that Franco came back and helped her across, steadying her with his strong hands.

After that the path lay around by the trees until the first slope came into view, covered in vines basking in the hot sun. Here and there she saw men moving along them, checking, testing. They turned to watch her and even at a distance she was aware of a strange *frisson* passing through them. One man looked at her in alarm and hurried away.

At last she reached the south slope. Here too there were memories everywhere, and she stopped to look around her. This was where she'd walked one evening to find Franco alone, and their brief tête-à-tête had been interrupted by one of his light-o'-loves.

Lost in her reverie, she didn't at first see the child appear and begin moving towards her, an incredulous expression on his face. Suddenly he began to run. Joanne smiled, recognizing Nico.

But before she could speak he cried, 'Mama!' and hurled himself into her arms, hugging her tightly about the neck.

Dismay pervaded her. 'Nico, I—I'm not—'

'Mama! Mama!'

She could do nothing but embrace him back. It would have been cruel to refuse, but she was in turmoil. She'd barely thought of her resemblance to Rosemary, and Nico had met her before. But that had been eighteen months ago, an eternity in the life of a young child. And the likeness must have grown more pronounced than ever for him to confuse them.

She should never have come here. It had all been a terrible mistake.

'*Nico.*'

The man had approached while she was unaware, and stood watching them. Rosemary looked up and her heart seemed to stop. It was Franco, but not as she had ever seen him.

The light-hearted boy was gone for ever, replaced by this grim-faced man who looked as if he'd survived the fires of hell, and now carried them with him.

He'd filled out, become heavier. Once he'd been lean and rangy. Now there was power in every line of him, from his thickly muscled legs to his heavy shoulders. He wore only a pair of shorts, and the sun glistened off the sweat on his smooth chest. An outdoor life had bronzed him, emphasizing his clear-cut features and black hair.

One thing hadn't changed and that was the aura of vivid life he carried with him, so that his surroundings paled. But it was belied by the bleakness of his expression.

'Nico,' he called harshly. 'Come here.'

'Papa,' the child called, 'it's Mama, I—I think—'

'Come here.' He didn't raise his voice, but the child obeyed him at once, going to his side and slipping his hand confidingly into Franco's big one.

'Who are you?' Franco whispered. 'Who are you that you come to me in answer to—?' He checked himself with a harsh intake of breath.

'Franco, don't you know me?' she begged. 'It's Joanne, Rosemary's cousin.'

'Cousin?' he echoed.

She went closer and his eyes gave her a shock. They seemed to look at her and through her at the same time. Joanne shivered as she realized that he was seeing something that wasn't there, and shivered again as she guessed what it was.

'We met, years ago,' she reminded him. 'I'm sorry to come on you suddenly—' She took a step towards him.

'Stop there,' he said sharply. 'Come no closer.'

She stood still, listening to the thunder of her own heartbeat. At last a long sigh escaped him and he said wearily, 'I'm sorry. You are Joanne, I can see that now.'

'I shouldn't have just walked in like this. Shall I leave?'

'Of course not.' He seemed to pull himself together with an effort. 'Forgive my bad manners.'

'Nico, don't you remember me?' Joanne asked, reaching out her arms to the little boy. A light had died in his face, and she could see that he did now recall their first meeting.

He advanced and gave her a tentative smile. 'I thought you were my mother,' he said. 'But you're not, are you?'

'No, I'm afraid I'm not,' she said, taking his hand.

'You look so like her,' the little boy said wistfully.

'Yes,' Franco said in a strained voice. 'You do. When my people came running to me crying that my wife had returned from the dead, I thought they were superstitious fools. But now I can't blame them. You've grown more like her with the years.'

'I didn't know.'

'No, how should you? You never troubled to visit us, as a cousin should. But now—' he gazed at her, frowning '—after all this time, you return.'

'Perhaps I should have stayed away.'

'You are here now.' He checked his watch. 'It grows late. We'll go home and eat.' He gave her a bleak look. 'You are welcome.'

Franco's workers gathered to watch them as they walked. She knew now why she aroused such interest, but still it gave her a strange feeling to hear the murmurs, *'La padrona viva.'* The mistress lives. Out of the corner of her eye she saw some of them cross themselves.

'They are superstitious people,' Franco said. 'They believe in ghosts.'

They'd reached the stream now and Nico bounded ahead, jumping from stone to stone, his blond hair shining gold in the late afternoon sun. It was the same colour that Rosemary's had been, as Joanne's was.

A man called to Franco and he turned aside to talk to him. Nico jumped up and down impatiently. 'Come on,' he called to Joanne, holding out a hand for her.

She reached out her own hand and felt his childish

fingers grip her. 'Hey, keep still,' she protested, laughing, for he was still bounding about.

'Come on, come on, come on!' he carolled.

'Careful!' Joanne cried as she felt her foot slip. The next moment they were both in the stream.

It was only a couple of feet deep. Nico was up first, holding out his hands to help her up. *'Perdona me,'* he pleaded.

'Of course,' Joanne said, blowing to get rid of the water and trying to push back wet hair from her eyes. 'Oh, my goodness! Look at me!'

Her soft white sweater had become transparent, and was clinging to her in a way that was revealing. Men and women gathered on the bank, chuckling. She joined in, sitting there in the water and laughing up into the sun. For a moment the light blinded her, and when she could see properly she caught a glimpse of Franco's face, and its stunned look shocked her. She reached out a hand for him to help her up, but it seemed that he couldn't move.

'Will anyone help me?' she called, and some of the men crowded forward.

'Basta!' The one word from Franco cut across them. The men backed off, alarmed by something they heard in his voice.

He took Joanne's hand and pulled her up out of the water and onto the bank. As she'd feared, her fawn trousers also clung to her in a revealing fashion. To her relief the men had turned their heads away. After Franco's explosion not one was brave enough to look at her semi-nakedness.

'I'm sorry, Papa,' Nico said.

'Don't be angry with him,' Joanne said.

Franco gave her a look. 'I am never angry with

Nico,' he said simply. 'Now let us go home so that you can dry off.'

'I went to the house first,' Joanne said, hurrying to match her steps to Franco's long strides, 'and the old woman there told me where you were.'

'That's Celia, she's my housekeeper.'

Celia emerged from the house as they approached and stood waiting, her eyes fixed on Joanne. She exclaimed over her sodden state.

'Celia will take you upstairs to change your clothes,' Franco said.

'But I don't have anything to change into,' she said in dismay.

'Didn't you bring anything for overnight?'

'I'm not staying overnight. I mean—I didn't want to impose.'

'How could you impose? You are family.' Franco spoke with a coolness that robbed the words of any hint of welcome. 'But I was forgetting. You don't think of yourself as family. Very well, Celia will find you something of her own to wear while your clothes dry off.'

Celia spoke, not in Italian but in the robust Piedmontese dialect that Joanne had never quite mastered. She seemed to be asking a question, to which Franco responded with a curt *'No!'*

'Your clothes will soon dry,' he told Joanne. 'In the meantime Celia will lend you something. She will show you to the guest room. Nico, go and get dry.'

It was the child who showed her upstairs, taking her hand and pulling her up after him. Celia provided her with a huge white bath towel and some clothes. She bore Joanne's garments away, promising to have them dry in no time.

An unsettling playback had begun in Joanne's head.
This was the very room she'd shared with Renata when
she'd first come here. There were still the same two
large beds, and a roomful of old-fashioned furniture.
As with the rest of the house the floor was *terrazzo*,
the cheap substitute for marble that Italians used to
keep buildings cool.

The floor-length windows were still shielded from
the sun by the green wooden shutters. Celia drew one
of these back, and opened the window so that a breeze
caused the long curtains to billow softly into the room.
Joanne went to stand there, looking out over the land
bathed in the setting sun. It was as heartbreakingly
beautiful as she remembered it, the Italy of her dreams,
blood-red, every colour more intense, every feeling
heightened.

She tried on the dress. It was dark, made of some
thin, cheap material, and it hung loosely on her slender
frame, evidently made for someone wider and shorter.
It was a pity, she thought, that Franco hadn't kept some
of Rosemary's clothes, but, after all, it had been over
a year.

And then, with a prickle up her spine, she remembered the words he'd exchanged with Celia. And she
suddenly understood that he did, indeed, have some of
Rosemary's clothes, and Celia had wanted to fetch
them, and Franco had forbidden it.

She went down to find Nico waiting for her at the
foot of the stairs. After the initial confusion he seemed
less disturbed than anyone at seeing his mother's image, and Joanne blessed the instinct that had made
Rosemary bring him to England. Clearly he remembered her from that visit.

He proved it by holding up a colouring book she'd given him. 'I've done it all,' he said. 'Come and see.'

He seized her hand and pulled her over to a small table in the corner. Joanne went through the pages with him, noticing that he'd completed the pictures with a skill unusual in children of his age. He had a steady hand, taking colours up to the lines but staying neatly within them in a way that suggested good control. It reminded her of her own first steps in colouring, when she'd shown a precision that had foreshadowed her later skill in imitating.

When they'd been through the book Nico shyly produced some pages covered in rough, childish paintings, and she exclaimed in delight. Here too she could see the early evidence of craftsmanship. Her genuine praise thrilled Nico, and they smiled together.

Then she looked up and found Franco watching them oddly. 'Nico, it's time to wash your hands for supper,' he said. He indicated the pictures. 'Put everything away.'

'Yes, Papa,' Nico said, too docilely for a child. He tidied his things and went upstairs.

'It's strange to find the house so quiet,' Joanne said wistfully. 'When I first came here there were your parents and Renata, with everyone shouting and laughing at the same time.'

'Yes, there was a lot of laughter,' Franco agreed. 'Renata visited us recently, with her husband and two children. They made plenty of noise, and it was like the old days. But you're right, it's too quiet now.'

'Nico must be a lonely little boy,' Joanne ventured.

'I'm afraid he is. He relies on Ruffo a lot for company.'

'Is Ruffo still alive?' she asked, delighted.

Franco gave a piercing whistle out of the window. And there was Ruffo, full of years, looking vastly wise because the black fur of his face was mostly white now. At the sight of Joanne he gave a yelp of pleasure and hurried over to her.

'He remembers me. After all this time.'

'He never forgets a friend,' Franco agreed.

She petted the old dog with real pleasure, but she also knew she was using him to cover the silence that lay between herself and Franco. She began to feel desperate. She'd known that Franco would be changed, but this grave man who seemed reluctant to speak was a shock to her.

'So tell me what happened to you,' he said at last. 'Did you become a great artist?'

His words had a faint ironical inflection, and she answered ruefully, 'No, I became a great imitator. I found that I had no vision of my own, but I can copy the visions of others.'

'That's sad,' he said unexpectedly. 'I remember how badly you wanted to be an artist. You couldn't stop talking about it.'

It was a surprise to find that he recalled anything she'd said in those days.

'I have a good career. My copies are so perfect that you can hardly tell the difference. But, of course,' she added with a sigh, 'the difference is always there, nonetheless.'

'And do you mind that so much?'

'It was hard to realize that I have no originality.' She tried to turn it aside lightly. 'Doomed to wander for ever in someone else's footsteps, judged always by how much I echo them. It's a living, and a good one sometimes. It just isn't what I dreamed of.'

'And why are you in Italy now?'

'I'm copying some works for a man who lives in Turin.'

'And you spared us a day. How kind.'

She flushed under his ironic tone. Franco plainly thought badly of her for keeping her distance, but how could she tell him the reason?

'I should have called you first,' she began.

'Why should you? My wife's cousin is free to drop in at any time.'

She realized that his voice was different. Once it had been rich, round and musical. Now it was flat, as though all the music of life had died for him.

A harassed-looking girl came scurrying out of the kitchen carrying a pile of clean plates, pursued by Celia's voice bawling instructions. The girl fled outside and began laying plates on the table.

'Despite the short notice Celia is preparing a banquet in your honour,' Franco informed her. 'That's why she's a little tense. My foreman and his family are eating with us tonight.'

'I love to remember the meals we had under the trees.'

'You were always nervous about the flowers hanging from the trellis. You said they dropped insects over you.'

'*You* did that. You slipped a spider down the back of my dress once.'

'So I did,' he said with a slight smile. 'That was to punish you for revealing to my mother that you'd seen me with a woman she disapproved of.'

'I didn't mean to betray you,' Joanne protested. 'It slipped out by accident.'

'I paid for your accident. My mother slapped me and

screamed at me. I was twenty-four, but that didn't impress her.'

They shared a smile, and for a brief moment there was a glimpse of the old, humorous Franco. Then he was gone.

'Why don't you have a look around, while I wash up?' he said. 'You'll find the house much the same.'

'I'd already begun to notice that. I'm glad. This was a happy place.'

She could have bitten her tongue off as soon as the words were out. It was as if Franco were turned to stone. His face was like a dead man's. Then he said simply, 'Yes, it was happy once.'

He walked away, leaving her blaming herself for her own clumsiness. This visit was turning into a disaster. Franco had said his foreman's family was eating with them 'tonight', which suggested that they'd been invited specially. Obviously her presence was a strain, and he needed some relief.

It had been madness to come here.

CHAPTER THREE

JOANNE wandered outside. The fierce heat of the day had subsided and a soft breeze had sprung up. At such times life at Isola Magia had always been at its most relaxed and contented, but now she could feel the growing tension. Even so, the beauty of the land struck her afresh.

Here was the terrace and the exact same place where Franco had nearly kissed her on that fateful night. Geraniums still hung from above, trailing in gorgeous purple majesty. A glance showed Joanne that it was the same plant that had flowered faithfully year after year, always putting forth the same beauty while life and death passed underneath.

There was the apple tree just under the window of the guest bedroom. Joanne had seen Franco stand beneath that tree on the night before his wedding, looking up at Rosemary's window. His bride had come to the window and gazed down at him with her heart in her eyes, and neither had moved for a long time. Joanne had crept away, feeling that it was sacrilege to watch.

She tried not to be self-conscious at the glances she received, wondering whether people were staring at her face or the unflattering dress. It was a relief when Franco and Nico emerged from the house and indicated for everyone to gather around the table.

Nico slipped his hand into Joanne's. 'Can I call you *Zia?*' he asked shyly, using the Italian word for 'Aunt'.

'I'd love that,' Joanne said. 'Will you show me where to sit?'

He led her to the table, and introduced her to everyone as 'Zia Joanne'. Umberto, the foreman, was there, with his wife and three children. The family greeted her politely, but with the look of awe that she was beginning to recognize. Franco sat at the head of the table, and Nico placed her between his father and himself. Franco poured her a glass of wine. His manner was attentive, but his eyes didn't meet hers.

As he'd said, Celia had whipped up a banquet in an amazingly short time, black olive pâté, spinach and ricotta *gnocchi,* and a delicious dish made of white truffles, the local speciality. It was washed down with the local wine.

Elise, Umberto's wife, had worked in the vineyards when Joanne had been there eight years ago, and remembered her. She questioned her politely, and Joanne talked about her career and her work in Vito's house. Franco spoke to her courteously, but she had the feeling it was an effort. Nico said little, but sometimes she turned and caught him smiling at her.

It was like floating in a dream. Everything that was happening was unreal. She knew every inch of this place, yet it was as though she'd never been here before. She knew Franco, yet he was a stranger who wouldn't meet her eyes.

But then she looked up and found that he'd been watching her while she was unaware. And there was something in his eyes that wasn't cold and bleak. There was despair and misery, reproach and dread; but also anger. For a moment his iron control had slipped and she saw that Franco Farelli was possessed by a towering, bitter rage.

Rage at what? At fate that had taken the woman he loved? At herself, for coming here and stirring up his memories?

She felt suddenly giddy. Heat rose in her, and she was transported back years to the last time she'd sat at this table, trying to hide her feelings for a man who didn't love her. There was a roaring in her ears and she felt as though the world were spinning.

Then it all stopped. Everything was back in its right place. Franco was talking to someone else. It might all never have happened.

But the soft pounding of her blood told her that it had happened. Nothing had changed, and yet everything had changed. He was no longer the fierce stranger he wanted her to think, but a man at the limit of his endurance.

At last Umberto and his family departed. The sun had sunk below the horizon, leaving only a crimson lining on the clouds, and that too was fading.

Celia appeared bearing a small tray with a bottle of *prosecco,* a very light, dry white wine, that was almost a soft drink. Italians drank it constantly, and Joanne even recalled being offered a glass as she had waited to be served in a butcher's shop.

Celia placed the bottle and glasses on the table, and added a little plate of biscuits that she set close to Joanne with an air of suppressed triumph. While Franco poured the wine she tasted one of the tiny biscuits, then checked herself.

'Is something the matter?' he asked.

'I'm sorry, I can't eat these. I'm allergic to almonds, and I'm sure I can taste them.'

Franco took a biscuit, tasted it, and frowned as he

studied the sugar coating. To Joanne's astonishment his
face grew dark with anger.

'*Celia!*'

The old woman came hurrying back. Franco asked
her a question in Piedmontese, and Celia answered with
a look of puzzled innocence. The next moment she
backed away from his blast of cold fury, and hurried
to snatch the biscuits from the table.

'What happened?' Joanne asked.

'It's nothing,' he said curtly.

'But you mustn't be angry with poor Celia just because I didn't like the food.'

'It wasn't that. Leave it.'

For the moment they'd both forgotten Nico, watching them with eyes that saw too much for a child. He
moved closer to Joanne and whispered, 'They were
Mama's favourite.'

Franco winced. 'Yes. I don't know what Celia was
thinking of. They haven't been served in this house
since—for over a year.'

'She must have thought that, since I'm Rosemary's
cousin, I might like the same things,' Joanne said
calmly, although she was feeling far from calm. She
suspected what Celia was really thinking, and it was
something far more eerie.

Franco seemed to pull himself together. 'Doubtless
she thought that,' he agreed. He was very pale. 'Nico,
it's time for bed.'

But at once the child squeezed closer to Joanne,
smiling up into her eyes. Instinctively, she opened her
arms to him, and he scrambled onto her lap.

'Let him stay,' she begged Franco. 'We used to cud-
dle like this when Rosemary brought him to visit me.'

'He was a baby then,' Franco said, frowning.

'He's not much more now. He's too young to do without cuddles.'

Franco sighed. 'You're right.'

Nico had dozed off as soon as he'd settled down, nestling against her. Joanne looked down tenderly at the bright head, and thought sadly of Rosemary who would never see her son grow.

'He's asleep already,' she murmured.

'He trusts you,' Franco said. 'That's remarkable. Since his mother died he trusts nobody, except me.'

'Poor little mite. Isn't there someone around here who can be a mother to him?'

'The servants make a fuss of him, but nobody can take his mother's place. Ever.'

Joanne turned her head so that she could brush her cheek against Nico's silky hair, and instinctively tightened her arms about him. Nothing was working out the way she'd thought. She'd been reluctant to see Franco again, fearing to be tormented by her old feelings. She hadn't allowed for the lonely child, and the way he would entwine himself in her heart.

'It's time he was in bed,' Franco said.

'Yes,' she said softly, rising with Nico in her arms. His head drooped against her shoulder as she headed for the stairs, and she smiled down at him tenderly.

Celia was upstairs, and darted away as soon as she saw her to open the door to Nico's room. Together they undressed the sleepy child, and slipped him between the sheets. He put his arms about Joanne again, and she hugged him back, her heart aching for the little boy who'd gone without his mother's embraces for so long.

'Will you sing to me?' he whispered.

'What shall I sing?'

'The song about the rabbit.'

For a moment her mind went blank. Then she remembered that Rosemary had written a little nonsense
verse that she'd sung to Nico. Gradually the words
came back to her, and she began to sing in a husky
voice.

'Look at the rabbit, scampering home.
See how his tail bobs, bobs, bobs as he runs.
It's late and he wants his supper,
Then he'll curl up and go to sleep.
And he'll snore, he'll snore, he'll snore.'

Nico gave a small delighted chuckle. 'Sing it again,'
he begged.

Obediently Joanne sang the little verse a second
time, and then a third.

'Again,' he whispered.

From the corner of her eye she could see Franco
standing in the doorway, keeping back, not to disturb
them. He didn't move or make a sound, but she was
aware of him with every fibre of her being, even while
she concentrated on the child.

It was just as well that she couldn't see his expression. It was that of a man in unimaginable pain.

She sang the verse twice more. Nico didn't ask for
it again, but nestled against her with a small sigh of
content. Thinking only to comfort him, she murmured,
'Buona notte, caro Nicolo,' as Rosemary had done.

'Buona notte, Mama,' he whispered, without opening his eyes.

'No, I—' she started to say, but fell silent, confused.
'Buona notte, piccino,' she said after a moment.

There was no answer. He lay heavy in her arms, and

very gently she laid him back against the pillow and kissed his forehead.

Then she turned to Franco. But he was gone. She didn't know how long he'd stood there before slipping away.

She closed the door quietly behind her and went downstairs. There was no sign of Franco, and she went outside onto the terrace.

There was a faint trace of light in the sky, but the land was dark, and she could see shapes only in outline. The air was heavy with the scent of flowers, as it had been on that summer evening long ago.

Franco appeared on the terrace and watched her for a moment as she reached up to the trailing geraniums.

'What are you thinking?' he asked.

'I was remembering these flowers from the night of the dance. Renata couldn't come, so we were going together. You waited for me just here, and when I came down—we talked.' She ended lamely, wondering if Franco would remember what had happened. His eyes were glowing and a gentle smile touched his lips.

'I remember,' he said softly. 'And while we were there Rosemary arrived. She came out of that door, and I saw her for the very first time.'

He'd forgotten Joanne's part in that night. His memories were all of his beloved. Joanne guessed that his meeting with Rosemary was so vivid in his mind that he saw nothing else at this moment. Just as he'd seen nothing else then.

'I should apologize to you for the trouble after dinner,' he said. 'Celia served that dish because it was a favourite of my wife's, although she hasn't served it for a year. I was angry with her because she seemed to think you were Rosemary's ghost. But I overreacted and I'm sorry.'

'It's not me you should say sorry to,' she reproached him gently.

'Don't worry. I've made my peace with Celia. She's very forgiving of my moods.'

'I expect you don't like to talk about Rosemary.'

'On the contrary. I love to talk of her, because that keeps her alive. But how can I? Sometimes Nico and I speak of her, but he's a child. I can't put too much on his shoulders.

'But you, Joanne—you were there the moment I met her, the moment I fell in love with her. They were the same moment.'

'I know. I watched the two of you look at each other, and it was as if the world had stopped.'

'That's how we felt too,' he said at once. 'She said so afterwards—as though the world had stopped. Or perhaps I said it to her, I don't remember. We were one heart, one soul—at least, so I thought.'

He said the last words half under his breath, then looked up quickly and caught her puzzled look. Before she could question him he hurried on, 'We knew everything from the first moment. And you were there. You knew as well.'

'Yes. Everything,' she said, with a touch of sadness that she knew he wouldn't hear. He was lost in his own world where there was only himself and his beloved wife. Joanne was a privileged guest, but only as a witness. She herself had no reality, and nor did her feelings.

'She came with us to the party,' she said. 'And you two danced every dance together. Other men kept asking her, but you growled and drove them away.'

'Yes, I did,' he said, with a smile. 'She urged me to do my duty and dance with other girls, but I said, "Only with you. And you, only with me. Always."'

'You asked Rosemary to marry you that night?' Joanne queried.

'I never asked her, and she never said yes. We simply knew it would happen. Some things are inevitable from the first moment.

'My mother couldn't understand that. She urged me to wait, to marry "a girl of my own kind", a good Italian girl. But Rosemary and I were soul of each other's soul and heart of each other's heart. And what could be more akin than that?' He gave Joanne a reminiscent smile. 'You saw it. It's almost as though you were a part of our love.'

She knew it was madness to go on with this. After all these years it still hurt to know that he saw her only through the filter of Rosemary. But it was sweet to sit here in the fading light, talking with Franco, feeling him turn to her, even if it was for the wrong reason. And she couldn't make herself give it up just yet.

'Why did you come back now?' he asked suddenly.

Caught off guard, she stammered. 'I—I was working in the neighbourhood. I couldn't leave without dropping in.'

'You avoid us for eight years, then pay a brief visit. Why, Joanne? Whatever did we do to offend you?'

'Nothing, it's just that my life has been so busy. My career—'

'Yes, yes,' he said dismissively, and she knew how tinny and dishonest her words had sounded.

'I should be going,' she said.

'It's much too late for you to start your journey now.'

'It's only sixty miles.'

'Surely you can stay for one night? Nico thinks you'll be here tomorrow.'

'But I've no night things, no change of clothes, nothing. I can't—' She looked down at the badly fitting garments.

'That was ill-mannered of me,' Franco said. 'Celia wanted me to lend you something of Rosemary's. I should have done so, but I was still confused by the sight of you.'

'You still have some of her clothes?'

'Come with me.'

The house was quiet as they passed through it. Joanne followed Franco up the stairs and along the passage to the room she remembered his parents occupying. It had changed little. The huge bed still stood there, with its bedhead of polished walnut. Two great closets stood on either side of the floor-length window with its wrought-iron balcony.

Franco opened the door of one of them, and inside Joanne saw a rail of garments protected by cellophane. Part of the closet was taken up with drawers which he pulled open to let her see the contents. Here were Rosemary's underwear, her nightdresses, scarves, gloves.

'I've given most of her clothes to charity,' he said, 'but some I've kept. Perhaps I should dispose of these too. I keep meaning to, but the moment never seems to be quite right. Take something to wear tonight.'

He walked out abruptly, leaving her to sort through the clothes. Every nightdress was filmy, delicate and low cut and they gave Joanne a glimpse into her cousin's marriage. The woman who had bought these seductive garments had known that her husband worshipped her body, and had wanted to present it to please him, just as she, Joanne, would have wanted to, if—

She shut that thought off. Rosemary might be dead, but she was still here, and Franco belonged to her as much as ever.

She ought to choose something plain and modest, but there simply wasn't anything like that. In the end she selected a nightdress of white silk with a matching negligée. She held the dress against herself, looking into the mirror. To her eyes her own face seemed pale and dull, almost plain. She was sure that Rosemary had looked more beautiful, her features illuminated by happiness.

She was so lost in her thoughts that she didn't hear the door open and Franco enter, nor see him as he stood watching her. Only when he came up close did she become aware of him.

'You startled me,' she said breathlessly.

'I'm sorry. Have you chosen something? Good. Why don't you take these too?'

He reached into the wardrobe and pulled out a set of riding breeches and jacket.

'I want you to stay tomorrow,' he said. 'We'll go riding and I'll show you what the place is like now.'

'I should leave,' she said, torn between longing and a sense of danger. 'I said I'd be back tonight.'

'Call your employers and tell them you're staying a few days.' It was a command, not a request.

She looked at him helplessly, torn by longing.

'Please, Joanne,' he said more gently. 'I haven't been at my best tonight. You took me by surprise and I've been surly and unwelcoming. Let me atone by being a good host tomorrow. And Nico so much likes having you here.'

She would stay for Nico's sake, she decided. It was good to have a reason that she could justify to herself.

'All right,' she said slowly. 'I'll stay tomorrow.'

'Thank you with all my heart. Let me escort you to your room.'

At her door he said gravely, 'Goodnight, Joanne. Until tomorrow.'

There was a phone by her bed. She called Maria and explained that she wouldn't be returning that night. When she'd hung up she slipped out of her clothes and put on the beautiful nightdress. She went to stand before the long mirror, and Rosemary looked back at her.

How had she missed the fact that the years had emphasized their likeness, fining her down, making her features more delicate, until she was Rosemary's image?

She shouldn't have returned. This place was too beautiful and heartbreaking. She almost wished she'd never seen Franco again rather than see him as he was now. There was only pain left in her heart. She knew it had something to do with the tortured man she'd met today. But she wasn't yet sure what.

She also knew that if she was wise she would leave this house as soon as possible.

But she wasn't wise.

Franco was late going to his bed. He wandered through the silent house, stopping outside his son's door and opening it a crack to listen to the soft breathing coming from inside.

He went to another door, and stood in darkness and silence for a long time before turning away.

When he finally lay down, sleep eluded him. His brain was in turmoil from the events of the day. Images came and went. One face in particular tormented him. He tried to shut it out, but it was always there.

At last he rose with a groan, pulled on a pair of jeans and went, barefoot, downstairs and out into the yard. There was a full moon, and its brilliant beams fell straight onto the tall window of the guest room. He could see that it was open, and for a moment he thought he saw a woman's form in a long white nightdress. But then he realized it was only the gauze curtains billowing softly in the breeze.

He stood watching for a long time, but there was no movement. At last he went to the fountain and sat on the stone, plunging his arms into the cold water, and laving it over his face. He was trembling.

'God forgive me for my thoughts!' he murmured. 'Merciful God, forgive me.'

CHAPTER FOUR

JOANNE was awoken by the sound of a cock crowing. A glance at her watch showed her that it was three in the morning.

That cock, she thought. It must be the same one. There can't be two with that weird sense of timing.

Eight years ago she'd often been awoken at this hour by the cock, which had then proceeded to crow every ten seconds. It might have been maddening, but, once she'd grown accustomed to it, it had ceased to bother her. Now, as then, she slipped back into sleep, with the crowing still in her ears.

Two hours later she awoke again. The cock had finished for the day and all was silence as she pulled back the shutters and stood looking over the vineyards.

Everything was magic. A faint mist rose from the land, and the soft grey light of dawn gave the world a ghostly appearance. From somewhere far across the valley a bell was softly tolling. Gradually the shapes grew firmer, the outlines more clear, and she became aware that a man was standing beneath a tree, looking out over the valley. She couldn't see his face, but she didn't need to. His height, the breadth of his shoulders, the carriage of his head, all proclaimed Franco. He stood easily, gracefully, oblivious to everything but the scene before him, gradually coming into view.

He was as motionless as a statue. Even as a very young man, she recalled, he'd had the gift of stillness. She wondered what his thoughts were now.

She backed into the room, lest he should turn and see her watching him. But he didn't move, and at last she went back to bed.

It was Celia who awoke her the next time, bustling into the room with a tray of coffee, and saying that *il padrone* wanted to make an early start. Joanne hastily showered and dressed in the clothes he'd chosen for her the night before. She was a little nervous about riding. It was years since she'd mounted a horse, and even then she'd been a cautious rider.

Franco was drinking coffee as she descended the stairs. He looked up, smiling, and she had a twinge of surprise. In contrast to the tense, anguished man of the day before he looked fresh and relaxed, and there was warmth in his eyes. He too wore riding breeches, with a white shirt that emphasized his tanned skin. The early morning sun caught the blue-black in his hair, his fine, clean profile and the sensual curve of his lips. Joanne could have enjoyed watching him all day, but she pulled herself together and managed to seem casual.

'Have some coffee,' he said, pouring it out. 'And then we'll leave at once. We can stop for something to eat on the way.'

'Where are we going?'

'I want to show you how the estate has grown. I bought some more land.'

The horses had just been brought round to the front. Her mount was a chestnut mare called Birba. She was beautiful, and seemed gentle enough, standing there quietly while Joanne mounted. But as soon as she was seated Joanne felt a tremor go through the animal, and recalled that *birba* meant 'little rascal'.

But the mare seemed to be on her best behaviour. Joanne's spirits soared as she rode beside Franco, out into the countryside, which was at its best. The sun was still climbing the sky and the day was no more than pleasantly warm. Across the valley she could see cypress and poplar trees, the red-tiled roofs of cottages, and acres and acres of vines.

'Franco, before we go anywhere,' she said, 'could you show me where Rosemary is buried? Is she in the churchyard?'

'No, we have our own burial plot. Come, I'll show you.'

He turned his horse through the little plantation that led from the garden at the back of the house, and down a path under the trees. From some distance away she could hear the gentle splashing of the stream, and suddenly they emerged into a small clearing.

Several graves stood here, but one was more recent than the rest. It stood close to the trees, a simple white marble headstone, surrounded by flowers. Willows hung over the water. It was a beautiful place, gentle and serene, where it was possible to believe that Rosemary lay sleeping in peace.

They dismounted, and Franco stood back with the horses as she neared the grave and dropped to one knee, touching the cool marble. Tears filled her eyes. Until this moment it had been almost as if Rosemary had slipped away somewhere, soon to return. But there was a finality about her resting place that brought the truth home to Joanne sharply. Forgetting Franco, she touched her fingers to her lips, then pressed them against the marble, murmuring, 'Goodbye, darling. Thank you for everything.'

When she turned around she saw Franco standing by the stream a few feet away. He looked up at her approach.

'Do you want me to wait for you?' she asked.

He shook his head. 'She'll understand. She knows I'll return another time. Let's go.'

He helped her mount, and wheeled his horse to the north. The air was brilliantly clear and she could see the snow-capped mountains in the distance. She delighted in the beauty of the morning and the nearness of the man who still had a hold on her heart. It was a different feeling from the joy he'd once inspired in her. But it was very real.

He'd extended the estate by a good deal, buying up land and varying his crop. Isola Magia had always grown the Barbera grape, used to make a delicious dry red wine. But now there was also the darker Barolo and the lively Brachetto.

'This was her doing,' Franco explained, showing her the rich vines with their burden of almost black grapes. 'Rosemary had a gift for business. She went into the details of the trade, and persuaded me to expand.' He grinned. 'My mother was very cross. She said Rosemary should stay at home and cook, though how she should do that when Mama wouldn't budge from the kitchen, I don't know. Then Mama said it was an insult to Papa, because he was still officially the head of the business.'

'I remember your father,' Joanne said. 'He was the most easygoing man I ever knew.'

'You're right. Of course he wasn't insulted. As long as he was free to eat and drink with his cronies he didn't care what else happened. Besides, his health was failing. He'd earned his retirement.'

'And you didn't mind Rosemary making changes in the business?'

'We were like one person,' Franco said simply. 'Where did she end and I begin? I never knew.'

They stopped at a small *taverna* and drank wines the innkeeper assured them were made with grapes from Isola Magia. They ate *antipasto piemontese*, served from a vast trolley that contained raw meat served with lemon juice and grated truffles, trout in aspic and meatballs.

'I can't eat any more,' Joanne protested.

'But that was just the starter.'

'It was a whole meal.'

'All right, we'll stop again later.' Franco toyed with his food a moment, before saying, 'You really loved her, too, didn't you? I don't think I quite realized that until today.'

'Yes, very much. We were very close for a long time.'

'Rosemary would speak of you as a sister, sometimes almost as a daughter.'

'That's how it felt to me too,' Joanne said slowly. 'I was six when my parents died. She asked her mother to let me live with them. I don't think Aunt Elsie was very keen. She was a widow. But Rosemary wouldn't give up, and I went to live with them. When Aunt Elsie died, she was only eighteen herself, but she became my mother.

'She was a wonderful mother, too. She should have been rushing around, dating, having fun, but she put it all aside to care for me. She lost heaps of boyfriends because she had me in tow.'

'Then I'm in your debt,' Franco said, raising his glass to her. 'You kept her free for me. What is it?' His sharp eyes had seen a change come over her face. 'You've thought of something. Tell me.'

'I suddenly remembered her gift for writing little daft verses—doggerel, she called them. There was one by my breakfast plate on the day of an important exam. It made me laugh, but it also made me feel safe and loved. Maybe that's why I sailed through the exam. Rosemary could do that for you.'

'Yes,' Franco murmured. 'She could.'

'Did she write daft verses for you too?'

He smiled. 'They used to fall out of my socks, usually when I was in a hurry. I didn't always appreciate them as I should. I used to say, *"Cara, please,"* but now there's nothing. If you knew what I would give for a piece of paper to flutter out of my sock drawer. Nico misses them even more. She used to sing her songs to him at bedtime. I'm glad you knew one last night. It meant so much to him.'

'Did she ever tell you that she longed to write a "real poem" one day?' Joanne asked.

'Yes, she did,' Franco said. 'She really wanted to achieve that ambition, but in the end she didn't manage it. "A poem that really meant something," was how she put it.'

'Everything Rosemary did meant something,' Joanne said. 'If it wasn't for her, I'd have been taken into care, and probably shunted around foster homes. She saved me from that, and I always promised myself that one day I'd do something for her, to thank her for everything.'

A strange note in her voice made Franco look at her curiously. 'And did you ever do so?'

'Yes,' she said, thinking of the years when she'd kept away from him, for fear of clouding Rosemary's happiness. 'I did.'

'Are you going to tell me what it was?' he asked after a moment.

'No, I can't do that. It was between Rosemary and me, and even she didn't know.'

'How close you two must have been despite the distance. You keep your secrets about her, and she kept hers about you.'

'What do you mean?'

'When she returned from seeing you in England, she said something very strange. She told me that at last she understood why you'd never come to see us in all those years.'

Joanne grew still. 'Did she tell you what she meant?' she asked, not looking at him.

'No. But she seemed happy about you for the first time. It had made her sad that you didn't visit, but not after that. She said that all the best she'd ever thought of you was true. Why was that? What happened between you?'

'Nothing special. It was wonderful to have her and Nico there. We talked and went shopping, watched television. Ordinary things.'

'You must have told her why you never came here.'

'But I didn't. It was never mentioned. Not once.'

'Then what did she understand? And how?'

Joanne cast her mind over those happy few days, but all she could recall were hours of innocent chatter about the little things that made up their lives, the comfortable feeling that they'd never really lost each other. After all the years their sisterly love had still glowed undimmed. Rosemary had talked of Franco with joy and pride. Joanne had rarely mentioned him.

Was it possible that somehow her cousin had divined

the truth? Was that why she'd said all the best she'd
thought of Joanne was true? The idea was breathtaking.

'What is it?' Franco demanded, watching her face.
'You've remembered, haven't you?'

'Franco, please, I can't talk about this. I may be
wrong—'

'I don't think so. You two understood each other.'

'Yes, we did. I'm only just realizing how deeply.'

He gave a wry grimace, and shrugged as he saw her
looking at him with a question in her eyes.

'It's nothing,' he said abruptly. 'It's just that—I'm
jealous. It's stupid, but I'm jealous. I don't like her
being close to anyone but me. Except Nico.'

'Do you know you talk of her in the present tense?'

'Do I? Perhaps. She's still very real to me.'

'Were you jealous when she was alive?'

'I'm a jealous man. What's mine is mine. Only she
never gave me cause. And I never gave her cause. I
claim no credit for that. I was never tempted.' He
drained his glass. 'If you're ready, let's go.'

Birba skittered a little as Joanne mounted. She'd almost forgotten that she was nervous of the mare, but
now Birba began to prance along, never quite out of
control, but never calm enough for Joanne to feel easy.

'Are you all right?' Franco asked.

'Fine,' she lied valiantly.

They turned back towards home and rode for an hour
before he stopped by a stream, saying, 'Let's rest here
for a while. The horses will be glad of a drink.'

As he spoke Franco was swinging himself to the
ground. Joanne was about to do the same when she
became aware of an ominous buzzing. A wasp was
circling her head. She swatted it frantically, but this
sent it fizzing near Birba's head, and suddenly the mare

reared, whinnying indignantly. The next moment she
was off, with Joanne clinging on for dear life.

She heard Franco shout behind her, but knew that
his chance of catching her was remote. He had to re-
mount before he could give chase, and Birba was
streaking over the ground at top speed. It was as
though, after being on her best behaviour all day, she'd
decided to shake off all restraint, and seemed to be
going faster and faster, soaring over hedges and ditches
as if they were nothing. Joanne was terrified, knowing
that she would fall off at any moment.

From somewhere behind her she heard the sound of
hoof beats and managed to turn her head just enough
to see a young man on a black horse, galloping hard
and gaining on her. Inch by inch he caught up, then
his arm came shooting out to go around her waist and
haul her off Birba and onto his own steed. She clung
to him thankfully, feeling the animal slacken pace,
while Birba tore on ahead.

'All right,' her rescuer said cheerfully. 'You're safe
now.' He finally pulled up.

'Thank you,' she said breathlessly, turning to face
him. The grin faded from his face, to be replaced by
shock. *'Rosemary!'*

'I'm not Rosemary,' she cried.

The horse had come to a halt. The young man
jumped to the ground and held up his arms to assist
her down. He held her for a moment, looking into her
face. He seemed to be in his late twenties, and was
extremely handsome, with a merry, mobile face.

'No, of course you're not Rosemary,' he said at last.
'She was an intrepid rider, and would never have lost
control like that.'

By now Franco had caught up with them. He flung

himself down from his horse and gripped Joanne's arm. 'Are you all right?' he asked hoarsely.

'I'm fine, thanks to—?'

'My name is Leo Moretto,' the young man said. '*Ciao,* Franco.'

'I saw what happened and I'm grateful,' Franco said, shaking his hand. 'It's good to see you back, Leo. Will you wait with Joanne while I recapture Birba?'

'Of course.'

When Franco had galloped away Joanne said, 'You knew her well?'

'I live around here. My father's land runs next to Franco's. We're old friends. And now tell me who you are, and how you come to be here in Rosemary's clothes, and with Rosemary's face? Am I seeing ghosts? Did I take a drop too much?'

His comical manner made her smile. 'No, of course not. I'm Joanne Merton. Rosemary was my cousin. I know we're very alike.'

'But only in your looks. What was Franco thinking of to let you ride Rosemary's horse?'

A shiver went through Joanne. 'Rosemary's horse?'

'Of course. That was her favourite mount. She often rode her when she went over the vineyard with Franco.'

'I see,' Joanne said in a colourless voice.

Franco was returning with Birba, now docile again. Leo hailed him. 'I was wondering what you were about, putting Joanne on that horse. She's only a moderate rider. Forgive me, Joanne.'

'No, it's true,' she said hastily.

'Of course,' Franco said. 'I should have thought. I had forgotten—a great deal.'

'We're close to my home,' Leo said. 'Come and

have some refreshment, and I can catch up with what's been happening while I've been away.'

'I don't think I want to get back on Birba,' Joanne said.

'Of course not, you'll ride with me,' Leo announced. 'Don't worry, you'll be quite safe.'

He sprang easily onto the animal's back, and drew Joanne up in front of him. At first she was nervous, but Leo's arm about her waist kept her safe.

The Moretto home was an old-fashioned farmhouse, sprawling and comfortable. Leo took them to a pleasant spot under the trees where there was a table, a couple of chairs and a swinging seat. He settled Joanne down on the cushions of the seat and promptly bagged the place beside her, leaving Franco to take the chair. The housekeeper brought out a tray with wine and cakes, and left them.

'Of course!' Joanne exclaimed suddenly. 'Now I remember you. At the *palio*. You and Franco collided.'

'*He* collided with *me,* and denied me victory,' Leo growled. 'There's a difference.'

'You rammed me to stop me passing you,' Franco said with a grin. 'But that's history. Now we're the best of friends.'

'Sure we are.' Leo smiled. 'And this year, I'm going to win.'

'If you don't lose your head,' Franco observed wryly. To Joanne he added, 'He's a madman when he gets on a horse.'

'I'm glad he is,' she said fervently. 'I've never seen anything like the way he galloped to my rescue.'

'The rescue of fair ladies is my speciality,' Leo said merrily. As he spoke he kissed the back of her hand with a flourish that was so gallant, and yet so droll, that she had to smile.

The two men, who evidently knew each other well, drifted into a discussion about crops, horses and wine. Joanne was feeling sleepy after her day in the open air, and she was content to sit there, letting the talk flow over her. When at last Franco rose to leave the light was fading fast.

Leo brought three horses out of the stables.

'You mustn't ride Birba again,' he told Joanne, 'so I've put your saddle on one of my own mares.'

'There was no need for that,' Franco said, sounding chagrined. 'I was going to ride Birba myself. Joanne would be perfectly safe on my horse.'

'She'll be even safer on mine,' Leo said smoothly.

They set off, Franco leading Birba, Joanne mounted on Leo's placid little mare.

'I'm sorry about that,' Franco said awkwardly. 'I gave you Birba without thinking. I'd forgotten that you weren't a confident rider.'

'It's all right,' she said hastily. 'After so long, how could you remember? And I managed her pretty well until she bolted, didn't I? Although not as well as—'

She bit the words back, regretting them as soon as they were out. A mood of contentment was enveloping her, and she wanted nothing to spoil this moment. As if he understood her thoughts, Franco nodded.

Riding home in the twilight, they began to talk of Rosemary again. Stories Joanne hadn't thought of for years came back to her, and strangely she found a measure of happiness in telling them, dwelling on Rosemary's memory. Franco said little, and once she fell silent, wondering if he could hear her, but he said urgently, 'Don't stop, I'm listening.'

'We're nearly home now. Nico will be waiting for us.'

'Celia will have put him to bed. Look at the time.'

'It's almost nine,' she said, astonished. Where had the time gone?

Celia was in the kitchen when they came in. 'Nico has been as good as gold,' she said.

'I'll go up and see if he's awake.'

Franco vanished upstairs and Celia indicated a spread of olives, meat, cheese and wine on the table.

'There is your supper,' she declared. 'And now, I go to meet my lover.'

She departed with dignity.

Franco came quietly down, smiling to himself. 'I looked in but he's sleeping like a log,' he said.

'Franco, Celia said she was going to meet her lover. At her age?'

'Don't be so prejudiced,' he told her with a grin. 'In this country we know there's no upper age limit to love. Celia's gentleman friend is a respectable man with a nagging wife who can't cook. Twice a week she goes to cook him a proper meal and "be friendly".'

'But where is his wife while Celia's doing this?'

'She goes to see *her* lover, of course. It's all very romantic.'

They laughed together and Joanne's heart eased.

CHAPTER FIVE

'LET'S eat next door,' Franco said, going into the next room, where the open fireplace had been stacked with wood. Now that the day's heat had faded there was a chill in the air, but he soon had a cheerful blaze going. Joanne carried in the food and laid it out on a low coffee table. They settled down on the huge sofa, and prepared to picnic.

'Oh, this is good!' she said, tucking into cheese and olives.

'Better than modern heating?' he teased, reminding her how she'd stared when she'd first seen the house's antiquated heating system.

'I wouldn't swap this for anything,' she said contentedly. 'I knew nothing in those days.'

He reached over and pulled a photograph album from a shelf, flicking through it until he found a large wedding picture, and gave it to her.

'Recognize yourself?'

'Is that me?' she asked, viewing the bridesmaid in horrified disbelief. 'I don't remember being as fat as that.'

'You weren't fat, just nicely covered.'

'I shouldn't have worn satin, though. Rosemary tried to talk me out of it, but the others were wearing satin, and I didn't want to be different.'

What did it matter what I wore when my heart was breaking? she thought. He had eyes for nobody but her, and poor Rosemary couldn't understand why I didn't care how I looked.

But the picture had explained something.

'I wasn't so like her then, was I?' she mused.

'You've grown more so with the years,' he agreed.

'No wonder you were shocked when you saw me yesterday. I shouldn't have appeared out of nowhere like that.'

'You gave us all a shock,' he admitted. He began to turn pages. 'Have you seen any of these others? I know she sent you some.'

She accepted his change of subject and went through the pictures. Some were familiar, but there were many she'd never seen before. She smiled as she went through page after page, but at the last page she stopped.

The picture showed Rosemary smiling with delight, her hands on her expanding waistline. She looked full of radiant health, yet the date underneath showed that the picture had been taken three days before her death.

'How could she look like that, and then—?'

'Her heart wasn't strong,' Franco said. 'Nico's birth weakened it. She should never have had the second child. God help me, I didn't know. If I'd known, I'd never have let her become pregnant again.' He added, so softly that she almost didn't hear, 'But she knew.'

'Rosemary knew she had a weak heart? And she didn't tell you?'

'She kept her secret until she had an attack on the day after that picture was taken. It was only a mild one, but the doctors told us that another could follow, and it would be fatal. On her deathbed she begged my forgiveness for deceiving me—' He broke off. 'As though there was anything for *me* to forgive. I longed to tell her of my gratitude for the years of perfect happiness, but no words would come.'

'I'm sure she didn't need the words,' Joanne said. 'When people are as close as you two were, they know, don't they?'

'I wish I could believe that she did. It has haunted me ever since.'

'Franco, Rosemary loved you with her whole heart. And she knew she had your love. If you could have heard the way she spoke of you when she came to England, if you could have seen what I saw in her eyes. But I can't believe you never saw that look. You must have seen it every day.'

'But you don't understand,' he said urgently. 'I thought I knew all this, until I discovered that she'd kept such a secret from me—from generous motives, I know. But I believed her whole heart and mind were open to me.'

'Is anyone's whole heart and mind ever open to anyone else, no matter how much they love them? Franco, people have to keep a little core of themselves *to* themselves. Sometimes even love can depend on that.'

'What a strange thing to say,' he said, looking at her.

'I know she loved you more than anything in the world, but she was Rosemary, a whole person. Not just one half of Rosemary and Franco. And that's how it should be. It's what made her special, made her the woman you loved.'

He seemed to relax. 'You're right, of course.'

It felt strange to be sitting here, explaining Rosemary to him, but nothing mattered now except to bring him some comfort. His sadness seemed to be her own, and if she could find some way to ease it she would. No matter what the cost to herself.

He finished the bottle and fetched another from the kitchen, refilling his own glass and hers. His eyes were a little wild.

'Do you do very much of this?' Joanne asked gently.

'Perhaps too much, at night, when there's nobody to see. I can handle the days, but the nights are very lonely. At first I thought I'd go out of my mind. A world without her was impossible, yet she was gone, so the world was mad. Or I was mad.

'They say time heals, but it didn't. The pain became different, that was all. For months I expected to meet her around every corner, and when she wasn't there she died for me all over again.

'I'd come home in the evening and listen for her voice in the silence, watch for her smile and know that I'd never see it again. I've wondered why I couldn't be like other men who put a dead love behind them. Why couldn't I let her go? What is the weakness in me that has clung on?'

'It's not a weakness to love faithfully,' Joanne protested. 'She was a special person. She deserved a special love.'

He was silent. He seemed to be struggling over a momentous decision. At last he said, 'I want to tell you something terrible, something I wouldn't admit to another living soul. I've actually blamed her for being better than other women, for giving me such happiness, then leaving me to spend my life in regrets.' He lowered his voice. 'I've almost hated her for leaving me. Can you imagine that?'

'Yes, I've heard of it before. It's natural—'

'Natural? To hate a woman because you loved her?'

'The greater the love, the greater the loss. You feel as if she abandoned you, don't you?'

'Yes. As she lay dying I begged her not to leave me, but she did. I know it wasn't her fault, but—' He clenched his hands as if fighting for the words. 'I blame her, and I blame myself for blaming her. In my mind, everything is tangled, and I can't see my way clear. I've just about worked out how to survive. And then you appeared...'

'I didn't mean to make it harder,' she said softly.

'I don't know whether you make it harder or easier. I don't understand anything that's happening.' He searched her face. 'Where did you come from?' he asked quietly.

'I told you—'

'I didn't mean that. I meant—' He drew a shuddering breath. 'Can you imagine what it was like to turn and find you standing there with *her* face? Like a ghost. Even now I'm not sure you're real.'

'I'm real enough,' she said, understanding him at last. 'Here, feel me.'

She stretched out her hand towards him, but he backed away, shaking his head, never taking his burning eyes from her. Impulsively she seized his hand, and held it firmly in hers. 'Feel me,' she repeated. 'Look at my hand. Hers were never like this. She had long, delicate fingers, like an artist, people used to say. But artists have powerful hands. Look how big and strong mine are. This is me, Franco, Joanne. Look and see *me*. Drive the ghosts away.'

He looked down at her hands in his, clasping them strongly. Joanne could feel the warmth from his body, sense the odour of earth and spice that was uniquely his. It affected her now as it had done long ago, and she wanted him now, as she had done then, so badly that it was an ache.

'Joanne,' he whispered. Then, more strongly, 'Yes, Joanne.'

He said it like a man awakening from a bright dream. She would have been hurt if she'd had any attention to spare for her own feelings. But they were lost in his. At that moment she would have made any sacrifice to give him a moment's happiness. Thinking only of that, she freed her hands and hugged him, holding him close as she would have done with Nico. And like his son, he held onto her for comfort.

'She's been dead over a year,' he said huskily, 'and every morning I wake up wondering how I shall endure the day. Only Nico keeps me sane.'

She stroked his hair. She was beyond speech. This was all she could give him.

'I begged her to return to me, and when I looked up and saw you standing there I thought—' A tremor went through him. 'I'm ashamed to tell you what I thought.'

'You thought it was her. And it was only me. I'm so sorry, Franco.'

'Don't be sorry. You gave me that moment, and it was more than I hoped for.' He ran a hand through his hair. 'What's the matter with me?' he said distractedly. 'Why can't I forget her?'

'Do you really want to do that?' Joanne asked softly.

He shook his head. 'Never. If the memory of her torments me to the end of my days, at least she's *there*. If I forget her, what would I do?'

Horrified, she searched his face, trying to find the words that would help his agony. But there was none.

Suddenly he burst out, 'Why don't you say it? You think I'm mad.'

'No, I—'

'The others do. They think I'm sick in my soul, as though a man must be mad to grieve for the love of his life. But they don't know—they can't understand—'

A shudder went through him and he seemed to control himself with an effort. 'I'm sorry. It isn't fair of me to burden you with this.'

'Why not? I'm here, and I only want to help you.'

Dumbly he shook his head, as though saying that there was no help for him. Forgetting everything but his need, she gathered him in her arms and held him tightly. His arms went around her, blindly seeking comfort, holding her to him fiercely.

It wasn't the way she'd dreamed of him holding her, but it was very sweet. She stroked his hair, murmuring incoherent words in which love and comfort were mixed. The years fell away. At this moment she was as much his as she had ever been.

'Hold onto me,' she whispered. 'Franco—Franco—'

He was quite still, as though trying to understand what was happening. When he moved, it was to draw back a little, just far enough for her to see his face, and the confusion in his eyes. He raised his hand tentatively, as if expecting a rebuff, and gently touched her face with his fingertips, the high cheek-bones, down the length of her face to the wide, full mouth, the resolute chin. She trembled at the touch she'd longed for and thought never to know. Looking into Franco's face, she saw something that made her catch her breath. Her heart was beating wildly. All the old bittersweet feeling welled up in her again, and it might have been yesterday that she'd stood close to him under the hanging flowers, longing for his kiss.

His hands were gentle, his fingertips featherlight.
She trembled at the sweetness of that touch. The next
moment his arms were about her and he was drawing
her close. There was a look in his eyes she couldn't
fathom, a look almost of desperation as he lowered his
head and touched her mouth with his own.

Her very bones seemed to melt. She clung to him
aching with desire and longing. After so many years
her dream had come true, and it was as perfect as she'd
known it would be. If only the world could stop at this
moment.

She felt his arms tighten around her, his mouth become more urgent. His desperate hunger communicated
itself to her through his lips, his skin, the heat of his
body. After that nothing could have stopped her. The
awareness of his need was like a match thrown among
straw. She pressed closer to him, reaching up to put
her arms right about his neck, eager and defenceless,
giving everything, holding nothing of herself back.

'Franco,' she whispered, 'oh, yes—yes—'

He covered her mouth again, silencing words. There
was nothing more she wanted to say anyway. There
was only this glorious feeling, and this wonderful man
for whom she'd waited so long.

His lips moved over hers hungrily, like a man who'd
found his dream after a long search. Thrilled, she responded to his urgency. The stifled passion of years
was welling up in her, making her press herself against
him, seeking to be closer and then closer still, seeking
to be one with him.

He wanted her. She could feel it in his movements
and the touch of his skin. Whatever happened afterwards, at this moment he wanted her as much as she
wanted him.

She reached for him, but he drew back a little, breathing hard. She could feel him shaking and thought she understood. But when she looked into his eyes, they were tortured. His hands were like steel, tensing against her, pushing her away.

'Franco—Franco—kiss me again—'

'No—I mustn't—I can't do this—forgive me—'

'There's nothing to forgive. Kiss me—'

'You don't understand,' he said hoarsely. 'I have no right—' He pulled away, staring at her with burning eyes. 'Forgive me,' he said again. 'I've behaved like a wretch. I'm worthless.'

'Franco, what are you talking about?' she pleaded, barely able to understand that this was really happening.

'I'm talking about my wife.' He rose abruptly as if he needed to put a distance between them, and turned away, running his hands through his hair. A terrible fear was growing in her.

'Don't you understand?' he said at last. 'Everything about today has been a fake. I've been with you, but I've seen *her*. It's her voice I've heard, her smile I've seen.'

She got to her feet and came closer to him. 'You mean I remind you of Rosemary, but I know that.'

'It's worse. *I've been pretending you were her.* I thought I'd learned to endure life without her, but when I saw you I yielded to a temptation so despicable that I'm ready to sink with shame.'

'But how could you pretend I was Rosemary? We talked about her. I said things she couldn't have said.'

'It's crazy, isn't it? But while we spoke of her, she was there with us. I could look at your face, and see

hers. Tonight, I wanted to kiss you, to feel you kiss
me—'

'Stop,' she cried desperately. 'I don't want to hear
this.'

'But you must hear, so that you may know never to
trust me. That's the only reparation I can make. Do
you want to know how low a man can sink when grief
has driven him to desperation? Then look at me, and
despise me as I despise myself.'

'Wasn't I—there at all?' she whispered.

'Yes,' he said after a moment. 'When you were in
my arms, you became yourself, and I understood the
terrible thing I'd done. To let you think I cared for you
when I cannot—when I *must* not—for pity's sake, go
away before I do something that's a betrayal of all three
of us.'

'You're talking in riddles. How could you betray all
three of us?'

'I would betray you with deception. I would betray
her if I cared about any other woman. I would betray
myself by letting my heart be false.'

'But why can't you care for another woman?' she
cried passionately. 'Rosemary doesn't need your love
now. I—' She bit off the fatal words there, praying that
he wouldn't have noticed. He seemed oblivious.

'We belonged only to each other, in life or in death.
She needs my love now more than ever, when the
world forgets and I'm the only one who truly remembers. I'm hers as I was when she lived, and I'll be hers
until the day I lie beside her.'

Joanne could bear no more. Blocking her ears with
her hands, she fled him. In her own room she locked
the door and threw herself onto the bed, sobbing bit-

terly, and trying not to hear the terrible words, 'I'll be hers until the day I lie beside her.'

She'd thought Franco lost to her from the day Rosemary had come into his life. But since Rosemary's death he was more lost to her than ever.

She heard him coming up the stairs and forced herself to be silent. He mustn't know she was weeping for him. She'd already allowed too much of her feeling to show, and wanted to sink with shame. His footsteps paused for a long time outside her door, while she held her breath. But then they went on, and faded away.

She went to bed, and lay staring into the dark, bleak with despair. The day they'd spent together had been so happy that it had sent her a little crazy.

But then Rosemary had appeared, just like before, and taken him from her. Because Rosemary was his true love, and no other woman existed for him. There was only the memory of his lips to torment her.

She fell into a restless sleep, and awoke in the small hours, feeling thirsty. She remembered the jug of milk that was always kept in the fridge. Slipping out of bed, she pulled on the negligée and made her way quietly out of her room, along the corridor and downstairs. The first light was creeping in through the shutters, touching furniture, vases. It was like creeping through a ghost house. The quiet was so profound that she could hear the faint whisper of the negligée trailing on the ground behind her.

She found the jug and poured herself a glass of milk. It was ice-cold and delicious. She rinsed the glass and turned to leave, but gave a little start of alarm.

Franco was standing in the doorway. In the semi-darkness she could see little more than his outline, but she knew it was him.

'You startled me,' she said. 'I was thirsty. I came down for some milk.'

He didn't reply. He only stood watching her with a terrible stillness.

'Franco,' she said with a touch of alarm. 'It is you, isn't it?'

'*Sì,*' he said in a strange voice. '*Son io. E te?*'

Joanne drew a sharp breath. Franco had replied, Yes, it is I. And you? But he'd spoken in Italian, when they'd been speaking English all day. Why should he suddenly fall into Italian, unless—?

Franco had told her that he wanted her to be Rosemary, and now she saw what he saw, a woman with Rosemary's looks, the slight differences concealed by the darkness, wearing Rosemary's nightdress. A slight shiver went through her.

He took a step closer to her, moving into a patch of light. He wore only a pair of shorts. She could see his bare chest rising and falling under the force of some tremendous emotion, and his eyes burned with a fierce and terrible fire. A man might look like that at a vision of hell—or the ghost of his love.

'*Perché?*' he said hoarsely. '*Perché adesso?*' Why now?

'Franco—listen—'

He silenced her with a finger over her lips. His eyes devoured her. She tried to speak but the hypnotic gaze of those eyes was too much for her.

Her mind protested that she must stop his delusion, for his sake as well as her own. But his gaze held her spellbound. In a trance she swayed towards him, feeling his hands on her arms, drawing her closer until she was pressed against him.

'*Mi amore…*' he whispered.

She whispered, 'No,' but no sound came. Her heart couldn't say no. Not after so long spent in hopeless longing. She knew this was dangerous. He'd warned her, but she couldn't be with Franco without wanting to be in his arms, whatever the risk.

'Mi amore,' she murmured in return. 'Heart of my heart…' The rest was lost against his mouth.

He kissed her fiercely, moving his mouth over hers with driving purpose, and she responded in helpless delight. Loneliness and sadness were forgotten. They might return a thousandfold later, but she would seize this moment and live on it for ever. If it was all she ever had, she would bear that somehow.

His own words of love had been spoken, not to her, but to the ghost who, for him, was still the only reality. The love she'd stifled for years had always been there, waiting to be reawakened by a touch. She still belonged to him.

He rained kisses over her face like a man possessed. Before there had been gentleness, but now his arms seemed to hold her a prisoner as his mouth traced a burning path down her neck. Her heart was thumping wildly as his caresses grew more intimate, and she arched against him, inviting his lips further. Her heart and her body had been parched for so long, and she had no strength to deny him now. If she paid for it to the end of her days, she would claim her moment and say that it had been worth any price.

He tossed away the negligée, leaving only the night-dress covering her nakedness. Beneath the flimsy material she was burning up. He'd warned her not to trust him, but that seemed so far away, in another world. She'd forgotten why she should be wary. She only knew that the thrilling sensations that were coursing through her made her feel alive for the very first time, and she wanted them to go on for ever.

Time vanished. She was a young girl again, vibrant with her first passionate love, joyful that the man she loved had taken her into his arms at last. It was as sweet and glorious as she'd dreamed, and there was nothing else in the world.

'My love,' she murmured. *'Mi amore…'*

The words seemed to pierce his delirium. His hands gripped her arms hard, pushing her away, and she saw his eyes, full of horror.

'Joanne,' he whispered. *'Joanne…* Dear God, what am I doing?'

The brutal return to reality made her freeze with shock. She wasn't his beloved, but an unwanted woman invading his grief. She had no right to his love, his desire, or any part of him.

'Dear God, what am I doing?' His words, but they could have been her own. Appalled, she looked down at herself, the thin material pushed awry, and she could have cried out with the bitterness of shame and rejection.

Franco was shaking, his face livid.

'For God's sake, go,' he said harshly. 'Go while you're safe. Do you hear me? *Go!* Never come back.'

CHAPTER SIX

JOANNE laid down the brush with relief. Her arm was aching from long hours of work.

'Come in,' she called to Vito, who'd looked in, a question on his face. 'I've just about finished this one.'

The easel bore a copy of a picture by Giotto, so perfect that only the most refined techniques could have revealed the difference. Vito whistled in admiration.

'Maria has sent me to bring you to supper,' he said. 'Now we will make it a big celebration.'

'Vito, please,' she said in a strained voice, 'would you mind if I didn't? I'm very tired. I'd like to go straight to bed.'

'You say that every night,' he said, scandalized. 'Since you came back, you do nothing but work and sleep. Maria cooks you lovely meals, and you don't eat them.'

Joanne smiled wanly. The elderly couple were full of kindly care for her, but all she wanted was to be alone. She forced herself to go down to supper and talk cheerfully. But as soon as she decently could she pleaded a headache and went to her room.

She'd been back two weeks now, and however hard she'd tried to pull herself together she was as devastated as she'd been the first day.

After the traumatic scene with Franco she'd rushed back to her room and dressed hurriedly. She hadn't been able to stay another moment in that haunted place.

Despite the darkness she'd run out to the car. Franco, sitting downstairs with his head in his hands, had risen to run after her.

'Joanne—please—not like this—'

'Don't touch me,' she'd flashed, throwing off his arm. 'Just get out of my way.'

He hadn't tried to stop her again, but had stood wretchedly watching as she'd revved up the car and turned it away from the house. She'd driven until she'd been sure Isola Magia had been well behind her. Then she'd stopped in a lay-by, rested her head on her arms, and sobbed without restraint.

It had all been her own fault. She'd known that. She'd gone where she'd had no right to be, and stolen love that had been meant for another woman. She'd been well repaid for her shamelessness.

She'd cried until she could cry no more. Finally, drained, she'd started up and driven slowly back to the Villa Antonini. She'd arrived in the early hours, before her employers had been up, and managed to escape to her room without needing to answer their kindly questions. Even so, when they'd met a few hours later, they'd been shocked at the sight of her distraught eyes.

Joanne coped by plunging into work, trying to smother the thoughts and images that tormented her. But she was haunted by Franco's tortured face, and there seemed no escape from the humiliation she'd brought upon herself.

She knew that Nico's birthday was due, and she bought a box of colours and mailed it to him with a loving note. She wondered if Franco would contact her to thank her, or at least to say something that would help take the sting out of their final moments together. Even if it was only to say a proper goodbye. But it was

Nico who wrote, in a childish hand, politely thanking her for the gift. From Franco there was only silence. Joanne tried to be sensible, despite the ache in her heart.

She found that one part of her mind could stand aside from her misery and judge the quality of her work, observing ironically that it was excellent. Her strokes had never been so precise, her colouring so exact. In her mood of self-condemnation she thought bitterly that her function in life had been underlined. An imitator. Second best. Someone with no true existence or voice of her own.

With the Giotto finished, she began preparing for the Veronese. While she was getting the canvas ready Maria looked in on her to say, 'You have a visitor.'

'A—?'

'A very handsome young man. Hurry.'

Joanne flung down her brush and tossed aside her smock, trying not to let her hopes rise. But she couldn't stop her heart beating eagerly as she ran downstairs.

Franco had come looking for her. Somehow, all would be well. She was smiling as she threw open the door. Then she stopped in her tracks.

Her visitor was Leo.

'I was passing through Turin, and hoped you wouldn't mind if I came to see you,' he said, with his attractive, boyish smile.

She pulled herself together and greeted him warmly, for she really liked him, and it wasn't his fault he wasn't Franco.

'You don't mind my calling?'

'Of course not, Leo. I'm glad to see you.'

She accepted his invitation to dinner that evening, and surprised herself by enjoying it. Leo's honest ad-

miration restored some of her perspective, and although
her heart still ached for Franco she began to feel more
able to cope. She reached home at midnight, which
Maria told her was ridiculously early.

'You should enjoy yourself more,' she said indignantly.

'Maria, he's only a friend.' Joanne laughed. 'He's
leaving Turin tomorrow.'

'He'll be back,' Maria declared. 'I see how he looks
at you.'

Leo returned a week later, asking her out so casually
that it seemed silly to refuse. But when he dropped in
again two days later she began to realize that Maria
had been right. There was a growing warmth in Leo's
eyes as he looked at her, and at last, over a candlelit
dinner, he said, 'I think I could easily fall in love with
you—with a little encouragement.'

He accompanied the words with a quizzical, humorous look, and she suddenly knew whom it was Leo
resembled. It was Franco as he'd once been, a boy
taking his pleasures lightly. Franco as he never would
be again.

'Couldn't you encourage me just a little?' he asked.

'I don't think I should,' she said, speaking lightly.
'You're probably really in love with Rosemary.'

'Why should I be?' he asked in genuine surprise. 'I
wasn't in love with her when she was alive. And you
aren't really like her, you know.'

'You thought I was at first.'

'Oh, your faces came out of the same mould, true.
But you're such a different person. She never attracted
me as you do.'

She could almost have loved him for seeing her as
herself, and not the pale shadow of her cousin. The

next moment he disconcerted her by asking, 'Is that what's the matter with Franco?'

'What do you mean?'

'Can't he free himself from Rosemary's ghost? The day I arrived you were hoping to see another man, one who made you smile. But the smile faded when it was only me. No prizes for guessing who you were expecting.'

'I wasn't expecting him,' she said hurriedly. 'In fact, I don't suppose I'll ever see him again.'

'Does he know you're in love with him?'

'No—that is—I didn't say I was,' she stammered.

'Do you think you had to say it?'

'It makes no difference,' she said despairingly. 'You're right. He's still in love with Rosemary. He always will be.'

'Has he no eyes to see?'

'Not to see me.'

'Then there's hope for me yet,' he said with a smile. 'You can't always love a man who's blind and stupid. One day you'll turn to the one who adores you.'

His manner was so light-hearted that she easily fell in with his mood. It would be pleasant to flirt with this delightful young man who knew the score and wouldn't expect too much of her. And perhaps, after all, he really might have the answer to her sadness. To forget Franco, and love Leo, who admired her for her own sake. As the wine grew lower in the bottle, and the candlelight flickered romantically, it became a tempting prospect.

He drove her back to the villa in his sleek sports car, and hand in hand they ran up the steps and into the house. In the dark hallway he whispered, 'Don't I get a little kiss, on account?'

'I guess you do,' she murmured.

She let him take her into his arms, hoping against hope that the vital spark would leap between them, freeing her heart from Franco. He pressed his lips to hers, kissing her gently at first, then with increasing warmth. He kissed charmingly, as he did everything, but she felt nothing. His arms tightened, he grew more ardent, and Joanne made no protest, hoping against hope that he could inspire her.

'Joanne, *carissima,*' he murmured. 'I adore you— and you feel something for me too, don't you? I can feel that you do—'

But he was deceiving himself. Her body, so eager and passionate for one man, was cold and dull for all others. She tensed, ready to pull away and tell him she had nothing to give. But before she could do so the hall light snapped on.

Franco stood there watching them, a grim, ironic smile on his face.

Joanne freed herself with a gasp. Leo grinned, his composure undented. '*Ciao,* Franco,' he said cheerily. 'But how awkward of you to be here just now. We were just getting to know each other.'

'Leo,' Joanne said indignantly.

'Forgive me, *carissima.* That was vulgar of me. But who knows where the night might have ended—?'

'I'm not interested in where your night would have ended,' Franco said coolly. 'Joanne, I need to speak to you urgently.'

He stood back and indicated for her to pass before him into the main room. Maria appeared and hijacked Leo. As Joanne passed she hissed into her ear, 'He came two hours ago, and said he'd wait however long it took. He's been sitting there looking like a thunder-cloud.'

Thundercloud was right, Joanne realized as she went to find Franco. Just why he should be angry was a mystery, but he regarded her low cut evening dress and glamorous make-up with hard eyes. She was determined not to flinch before his disapproval, and she walked past him into the room, tossing aside her evening cloak to reveal her bare shoulders. Then she faced him, hoping her inner disturbance didn't show in her face.

'What did you want to say to me?' she asked, and to her relief her voice sounded cool and in control.

'A great deal,' he replied, looking her up and down. 'But much of it has gone out of my head. It's a surprise to find you in Leo's arms.'

'Then you've got a nerve,' she said with a flash of temper. 'It's no business of yours who I go out with, or who I kiss.'

'Of course. I merely thought you had better taste.'

'But Leo's a friend of yours.'

'That doesn't make him a suitable friend for you. He's a playboy, a Lothario—'

'He's fun. We have a great time together.'

'Evidently,' he snapped.

'Franco, I don't know why you came, but if it was just to criticise my friends you can leave again.'

'I came to take you back to Isola Magia. Nico has set his heart on having you there for his birthday tomorrow. I've cleared it with your employers.'

She drew a long breath as the memory of the last few miserable weeks rose. He'd ignored her, then felt he could snap his fingers for her return. Joanne seldom lost her temper, but she lost it now.

'I'm sorry you had a wasted journey, Franco,' she said firmly, 'but I'm very busy for the next few days—'

'I told you I'd cleared it with your employer—'

'But you neglected to clear it with me. I do have some feelings.'

'And evidently they're all tied up in Leo Moretto,' he said in a tone that was almost a sneer. 'What a pity you don't have your cousin's clear sight. Rosemary always said he was so shallow that you could see right through him.'

'Rosemary was in love with you,' Joanne said defiantly. 'But I'm not her. I'm Joanne, and my tastes are my own.'

Franco gave her a strange look, and she guessed he was remembering how she'd betrayed herself in his arms, wondering how much her actions had meant then, how much her words meant now.

'I don't ask for myself,' he said at last, 'but for my son. You won Nico's heart. Do I have to tell you how precious a gift that is? Did you delight him only to amuse yourself, and to throw him aside when it suits you?'

'Of course not. That's a wicked thing to say.'

'Then come back with me now. It will mean the world to him—and to me.'

'To you?' she echoed uncertainly.

'Nico is all I have left to love. Last year his birthday was sad, coming so soon after his mother's death. This year I want him to enjoy himself as a child should, and you can give him that.' When she hesitated he burst out, 'Do you think it was easy for me to come here and see you again?'

'No, I don't. Any more than it's easy for me to see you.'

'Yes, it's hard for both of us, but can't we put our differences aside for the sake of that little boy?'

'Of course we must,' she said after a moment. 'I'll come with you first thing tomorrow.'

'I'm afraid we can't wait until tomorrow. I promised Nico you would be there when he awoke.'

'You *promised* him—?'

'I knew I could rely on your kindness.'

'You knew nothing of the sort,' she said indignantly. 'You relied on being able to steamroller over me. Obviously Rosemary let you dictate to her—'

'Rosemary would never have argued where Nico's happiness was concerned,' Franco told her quietly.

That silenced her.

'It hurt him to awake and find you not there that morning,' Franco said. 'He kept asking why you'd gone without saying goodbye.'

'I wonder what you told him,' Joanne flung at him. He had the grace to redden.

'Please, Joanne, let's forget that. What happened was my fault, and you have every right to be angry with me. But if I promise you that it won't happen again— please, for Nico's sake.'

She knew his words were meant as reassurance. It was as well that he didn't know the hurt he was giving her. How could she have thought there could ever be anything between her and Leo when Franco could affect her like this?

She thought of returning to Isola Magia with him, being close to him, knowing that he was keeping his distance, having to hide her feelings. And her mind cried that she couldn't do it. But her heart couldn't resist another day with him, even on these bitter terms.

And there was Nico, the bright-faced little boy

who'd come so trustingly into her arms. How could she disappoint Rosemary's child?

'All right, I'll come.'

'Thank you,' he said fervently. 'We'll leave as soon as you've changed. Can you hurry, please?'

'I'll need time to pack an overnight bag.'

Franco look awkward. 'I hardly know how to tell you this, but Signora Antonini is very kind-hearted, and when I told her the reason for my urgency she packed your bag herself.'

'Really,' Joanne said, almost bereft of speech. 'Well, you've certainly left me nothing to do.'

It seemed that Maria was not merely kind but romantic. She met Joanne on the landing, her eyes shining.

'Two lovers,' she pronounced triumphantly. 'How exciting!'

'He's not my lover,' Joanne protested.

'Nonsense, of course he is. When you were so late getting home he was very upset. You take him. He's worth ten of that other one.'

It was pointless arguing. Joanne changed out of her glamorous evening dress and went downstairs. Franco was waiting impatiently by the front door. Leo lounged around in the hallway, regarding Franco ironically.

'What a shame our evening ended so abruptly,' he said to Joanne. 'But I'm going home myself tomorrow, so I dare say we'll meet again soon.'

'I won't be there long,' Joanne said quickly. 'Maria, I'll hurry back to work.'

'You stay away as long as you like,' Maria told her. 'A pretty girl like you should enjoy herself with all her lovers.'

'Shall we go?' Franco asked.

He had a large, heavy-duty four-wheel-drive car, useful for the estate, and totally different from Leo's showy sports car. He put Joanne's bag in the back, asked if she was comfortable, and started up.

When he'd driven for some time in silence, she said, 'I can't help Maria talking like that. I've told her we're not lovers, but she is the way she is.'

'You don't have to explain Maria to me. I have several aunts just like her.'

'I didn't want you to think that I gave her the impression that we—'

'I probably did that. I was annoyed not to find you there, and I'm afraid it showed, especially when you were so late. I was beginning to think you'd be out all night.'

'It's not as late as that.'

'You came in at nearly two in the morning.'

'Goodness, I hadn't realized.'

'No, I understand Leo can be charming company. We shouldn't find too much traffic at this time of night. We'll be there soon and you can get some sleep.'

She didn't react to his abrupt change of subject. She sensed that beneath his courtesy Franco was angry. But he had no right to be.

The world seemed to be whirling around her. Only a short while ago she'd thought she would never see him again. Yet here she was, sitting beside him as they drove through the night.

They were soon off the main roads and out into the country, where there were no street lamps, and little passing traffic. By turning her head slightly she could see his face, almost in darkness, except that the lights from the dashboard threw him into relief. He looked like a man made of bronze. His only movement was the occasional turn of the wheel. He stared straight ahead, almost as if she weren't there.

Her annoyance returned. She'd fought so hard to put him out of her mind. But when he turned up, practically commandeering her, she knew that all the work had been in vain. She was as much in love with him as ever. And he ignored her.

'I'm sorry you had a long wait,' she said coolly. 'Perhaps if you'd called me first—'

'I couldn't. Nico asked for you tonight, as he was going to bed. I didn't know where you were. You left no address. You'd mentioned only your employer's name and that he'd made his money in engineering. I had to do some fast detective work.'

'And tomorrow wouldn't have been good enough?'

'That's right.'

'Franco, are you sure this is a good idea? You know why Nico wants me, to fantasize that his mother's returned. Is it wise to indulge that fantasy? He could suffer for it later—'

'You're wrong,' he interrupted her. 'It's "Aunt Joanne" he wants. You can talk to him about Rosemary. He's thrilled about your connection with his mother, but he knows who you are. Nico is less confused about you than—than anyone else.'

He stopped talking abruptly, as though afraid of what he might be betrayed into saying.

As they neared Isola Magia he slowed, and by the time they approached the gate the car was crawling along. Once inside he stopped the engine while they were still some distance from the house.

'I'm afraid we have to walk from here,' he said. 'If I drive closer Nico will hear us. I told him he'd simply wake up tomorrow and find you there, like magic. If

he knows when you arrive tonight it will spoil it for
him.'

'But surely he knows why you went out?'

'I left after he went to sleep. With luck he may never
know I was gone. I promised him that you would appear "like magic", and that's what I want to happen.
He's lost so much. I want to please him.'

She was touched by the imaginative way he'd
thought himself into the child's mind. Beneath the hard
shell with which Franco protected himself, there was
still a loving heart, even if it was only for a little boy.

A moon had appeared, and by its light Joanne could
see the house, a dark bulk, a few hundred yards away
among the trees. She could just make out the path at
her feet.

'Be careful, the ground is uneven,' Franco said.

She trod carefully, wishing she could see more
clearly, but then the moon went behind a thick cloud,
and suddenly she was in total darkness. Her foot went
down into a rut. She gasped and staggered, almost falling. But strong hands came out of the darkness, to hold
her. She clasped him frantically back and felt herself
held firmly against his chest.

'Steady,' Franco said in a ragged voice. 'Are you all
right?'

'Yes—yes, I'm all right.'

Silence fell between them. He didn't release her, and
suddenly she knew that he couldn't make himself do
that. He was trembling, and beneath the thin material
of his shirt she could feel the thunder of his heart.

She looked up. She couldn't make out his face, but
she could see his eyes glittering strangely, and heard
the sharpness of his breathing. He wanted to kiss her,
wanted it desperately. She knew that because it mir-

rored her own desire. His hands on her arms tightened, drawing her closer. In another moment he would lower his head.

'The moon's appeared again,' he said raggedly. 'You'll manage better now.'

She was still standing with him, yet nothing was the same. As though a curtain had been ripped aside she saw the truth behind his outward calm. He wanted her, yet he was determined not to want her. He'd vowed to set a distance between them, and he would keep that vow, no matter how it tormented him. He saw her only as the reincarnation of his dead wife, and there would be heartbreak—for both of them—in pursuing that delusion.

She understood this as she stood there, held against his chest, feeling the heat from his body, and her anger with him grew for the way he could provoke her feelings without returning them. She pulled herself free.

'I can walk, thank you,' she said coldly.

Luckily the moon appeared again and she was able to make her way to the house unaided. As they neared it they saw a light coming from Nico's room.

'Quickly, come into the trees,' Franco whispered. 'He mustn't see us.' He put out a hand to guide her, but immediately drew it back.

They moved into deep shadow, looking up at the window where the light still glowed.

'He must have awoken,' Franco said. 'I hope he hasn't discovered that I've gone. Celia promised not to go to bed until I returned.'

They were still, waiting, holding their breaths. Overhead the stars swung in silent majesty, and all the world seemed to be still.

'Try not to hate me, Joanne,' he said sombrely. 'You

have every right, after the way I behaved. But don't let Nico be hurt, I beg of you.'

Hate and anger were only different sides of love. Being with him had taught her that, but she couldn't tell him so.

'I'll never do anything to hurt that little boy,' she said. 'That's why I'm here.'

'That's all I ask. His light's gone out. Let's get inside quickly.'

They crept noiselessly into the house and up the darkened stairs. A floorboard creaked, and they stood petrified. Then they heard footsteps from behind Nico's door. At once Franco moved forward and opened the door. Joanne heard Nico's glad cry of 'Papa!' and a grunt as though they'd clasped each other vigorously.

'You should be in bed,' came Franco's voice.

'I was coming to see you. Is Aunt Joanne here yet?'

'She'll be here when you wake up tomorrow. My word on it!'

'Why not now, *now?*'

Franco spoke in a strange, constricted voice, 'Is it so important that she comes here?'

'But you like her too, don't you, Papa?'

'Go to sleep, my son,' Franco said heavily after a moment. 'Wait for the morning, and see if I've kept my word.'

'Will it be my birthday soon?'

'It'll never be your birthday if you don't go to sleep,' Franco said firmly.

'I'm asleep now,' Nico insisted at once.

To her surprise Franco chuckled. It was a rich sound that touched her senses. Keeping well back, she moved across the door until she could see inside the room.

Franco had lifted Nico in his arms and was setting him down on the bed. 'Snuggle down now,' he said.

His voice was gentle, patient, full of love. Nico wriggled down in the bed and Franco tucked in the sheets around him.

'You're not cross because I was awake?' Nico asked sleepily.

'No, my son. I'm not cross with you.'

He leaned down and kissed the child. Joanne moved back slowly, careful not to make a noise. At last she gained the room that had been hers last time, and slipped inside. Just before she closed the door she saw Franco come out into the corridor and stand in a patch of moonlight. As she watched, he dropped his head and covered his eyes with one hand. He looked like a man at the end of his tether.

If only she could go to him now, put her arms about him, tell him that she loved him and longed to comfort him. But she knew he couldn't cope with that.

He raised his head, and for a moment she thought she saw the glint of tears on his face. Joanne backed silently into her room, and closed the door.

A moment later there was the sound of a soft tap and she heard Franco's voice. 'May I come in?'

'No,' she said quickly. 'I've gone to bed.'

'Is there nothing you want? Some refreshment?'

'Nothing,' she said, trying to keep her voice steady. 'Please go away, Franco. Please.'

CHAPTER SEVEN

JOANNE was up early, ready and dressed before Franco came for her.

'Thank you,' he said. 'After that late night, I'm impressed.'

Joanne smiled. 'I know what children are like on birthdays.'

Franco was dressed in jeans and an olive-green vest. His brown arms were glistening as if he'd already been outside working. To the casual glance he looked as if he didn't have a care in the world. Only a certain tension around his mouth hinted at the truth.

They were just in time. Further along the corridor they heard Nico's door open and a small voice say, 'Papa?'

'Here!' Franco called cheerfully.

The next moment Nico saw Joanne and his face lit up. Still in his pyjamas, he raced at her full tilt, almost knocking the breath out of her as they collided.

'*Zia, zia!*' he squealed. 'You came!'

'Of course I did,' she said, laughing. 'Oof! Don't strangle me.' Nico had leapt up into her arms, hugging her tightly around the neck. She kissed him back and rubbed her cheek against his shining hair.

'Happy birthday, little one,' she said.

'You weren't here when I went to bed?' he said, making the statement a question.

'I came in the night, when you were asleep,' she declared dramatically.

'But what made you come?' he asked, taking her by surprise.

Joanne thought fast, dropping down on one knee to look the child in the eyes. 'I knew you wanted me,' she said. 'That was all I needed to know.'

'But how did you—?'

'Shh!' She put a finger over her lips. 'It's magic, and we mustn't talk about it.'

He beamed at her. 'This is going to be the best birthday *ever.*'

'Don't I get a kiss too?' Franco demanded, laughing.

Nico hugged his father, bouncing eagerly and carolling, 'I'm seven, I'm seven.'

'Almost a man,' Franco teased.

'Will I be a man next year, Papa?'

'Very soon,' Franco promised.

'*Zia,* come and see my puppies,' Nico begged, seizing her hand and pulling her downstairs.

'How about getting dressed first?' Franco called.

'I must see the puppies first, Papa.'

'How long have you had them?' Joanne asked, following him breathlessly downstairs.

'Celia gave them to me yesterday.'

The little dogs were older than Joanne had expected, being about four months. Both were female. One was covered in long fur and looked like a mop. Nico had named her Zazzera, shock of hair. Zaza for short. The other was smooth-haired with an excitable temperament, so Nico called her Peperone. And she became Pepe.

'Celia's brother has a little farm near here,' Franco said, catching up. 'As a sideline they breed dogs, to sell in the markets. But males sell faster than females.

These two have been to market and back seven times, and nobody was going to give them an eighth chance.'

'They were going to kill them,' Nico said earnestly. 'So I asked Papa and he said I could have one. But I couldn't take just one and leave the other one to die, could I, *Zia*?'

'No, you couldn't do that,' Joanne agreed, regarding him tenderly.

Without warning there were tears in her eyes. She rose hastily and went out onto the terrace. Nico was embracing his pets again and didn't notice, but after a moment Franco followed her.

'What is it?' he asked urgently.

'Nothing, I just—I suddenly remembered Rosemary, when she telephoned me to say she was pregnant again. She was so happy, and she said she was glad Nico would have a little brother or sister before he was seven. I can hear her saying, "That's just the right age gap. He'll be old enough to learn by being close to a small, helpless creature." She'd be so proud of him today.' She wiped her eyes. 'I'm sorry.'

'Don't be sorry for loving her,' Franco said. 'How could anyone not do so? I only hope I can raise her son to be worthy of her.'

'You're doing a wonderful job with him. He's a splendid little boy.'

'Yes, he is, isn't he?' Franco's eyes shone with love and pride. Joanne looked away, realizing that today was going to be harder than she'd thought.

But despite her fears, breakfast was a cheerful meal, out under the trees, with Pepe, Zaza and Ruffo crouched beneath the table, poised for titbits. Celia served it hastily, for she was already deep in preparations for Nico's birthday party that evening. Even

Franco, venturing to look into the kitchen, had been driven out by Celia's indignation.

Nico ate his breakfast in a state of suppressed excitement, throwing his father significant looks.

'Have I forgotten anything?' Franco asked at last, all bland innocence.

'Papa!' Nico protested indignantly.

'Oh, your present. Well, let me see, it's a bit late to be thinking of anything—' His eyes were full of mischief.

'Papa!'

Franco laughed. 'Let's see what's hiding around the corner of the barn.' He raised his voice. 'All right, you can bring him out.'

A grinning young man came around the barn, leading a small, fat pony. Nico's shriek of delight made everyone cover their ears. Leaving the rest of his breakfast untouched, he bounded over to throw his arms around the pony in an ecstasy of love.

'He's so like his mother,' Franco said in a low voice. 'She too was always full of eagerness.'

'I remember you as just the same,' Joanne said impulsively. 'When I first met you all those years ago you seemed to regard all life as your own to be enjoyed.'

'I was a heedless boy then, taking everything because I thought my own pleasures mattered. She taught me better.'

Nico's eager shouts recalled him to the present. Smiling, he helped his son into the saddle, and led the pony around the yard. Nico sat holding the rein with the confidence of a child who had already learned to ride, while the pony ambled placidly along. Pepe and Zaza gambolled at his heels, but he ignored them.

'Papa says we can all go riding together,' Nico said, scampering back to her.

'I promise you a slower horse today,' Franco said instantly.

'So I should hope.'

'Can we go *now?*' Nico begged.

'Just as soon as we've changed,' Franco promised.

'I'm going to change,' he called, already halfway to the house.

Left alone, Franco gave her a wry look. 'You don't mind, do you?'

'I'm here to do whatever pleases Nico.'

When she came down a few minutes later, wearing Rosemary's riding things, she was glad to see that she did indeed have a quieter-looking horse. Nico was already mounted and eager to go. He flapped the reins and urged his mount on, but the placid little pony moved at a sedate pace.

'Papa, he won't go fast when I tell him to,' Nico cried indignantly.

'Thank heavens!' Franco declared wryly. Under his breath he added to Joanne, 'The man who trained him promised me that.'

She chuckled and they shared a smile. Franco seemed to be growing more relaxed, almost contented when his eyes rested on his little son.

They descended into the valley and began to climb the other side, passing through little villages. In one of these they found a small inn and sat outside at a table beside a wooden rail, looking down into the valley, where they could see Isola Magia, basking in the sun. At this distance it looked peaceful and content.

The landlord brought Nico a milk shake. The others drank *prosecco* with sweet biscuits.

'What is it, Nico?' The child was tugging at his sleeve. He whispered something that made Franco frown and shake his head. 'No, *piccino*. Not this year.'

'But we didn't go last year, either,' Nico pleaded. 'And *Zia* could come too—'

'No,' Franco said, more sharply than Joanne had ever heard him speak before. He softened the effect by squeezing the child's shoulder, but Nico still looked upset.

'What is it?' Joanne asked.

'Nico wants to go to Lake Garda,' Franco explained. 'I have a little villa there and we've always visited it in summer, except for last year. The time isn't right yet, Nico.'

'I'm sorry, Papa,' the little boy said, with a gentleness that made him seem much older than seven. He squeezed Franco's hand between his own small ones. 'It'll be all right, Papa. Truly it will.' For a moment it was he who was offering comfort.

And it was there again, the echo of Rosemary saying, 'Don't worry, I'll look after you,' as Rosemary had said so often in the past. 'Don't worry, I'll take care of you—I'll be your sister, your mother—'

And she'd repaid Rosemary's bounty by wanting her husband. Driven by the need to get away from the other two, she rose quickly and went to stand by the stone wall, looking out at the view.

After a while there was a touch on her shoulder.

'I'm sorry to force that on you,' Franco said. 'Please believe I didn't plan it. I've commandeered your day, but I couldn't ask for a whole week.'

'I don't mind if it will make Nico happy.'

'If I could persuade him to choose somewhere else—'

'But he wants to go there,' Joanne said. 'He was happy there, with the two of you. You're right. It's not a good idea. You should take him there some time in the future, but without me.'

He was silent so long that she turned to look at him, and something she saw in his eyes made her heart beat rapidly.

'Without you?' he echoed quietly.

'What do you think I am?' she demanded. 'Just a doll with Rosemary's face? I'm Joanne. You want me to be a copy of Rosemary, like the imitation pictures I paint. On the surface, everything looks the same, but it's all false. At least Leo—'

'Must we talk of him?' Franco demanded sharply.

'Leo sees me as *me*. I like him for that.'

Franco's lips tightened. 'I think we should return home now.'

They made their way back slowly, Nico riding between them. He talked non-stop, relieving them of the task of appearing normal. It was a relief to them both when the house came into view.

Everything was ready for the party, and soon the guests and their parents began to arrive. Joanne was swept up in the merrymaking. She helped serve the refreshments, took part in the games, and met many of the neighbours, trying not to see the strange looks they gave her and Franco.

But, although she seemed oblivious to him, she was acutely aware of Franco all the time. He too played games and joined in the songs, apparently enjoying himself. Joanne guessed what it must cost him to appear cheerful when he must be recalling other parties, with his wife. But he allowed no sign of his own sadness to appear.

As the light faded coloured lamps came on in the trees, and those who could do a turn were pressed into service. An old man played an accordion, two little girls did a dance, a boy did a recitation, all to great applause. Someone called for Nico to sing, but the little boy refused bashfully.

'He must sing,' Celia confided to Joanne. 'He has a lovely voice.'

The calls grew. Nico continued to shake his head, and hid his face against his father.

'It's your birthday, my son,' Franco chided him gently. 'Your guests have brought you gifts. Now you must do what pleases them.'

'I can't sing alone, Papa,' Franco pleaded. To Joanne's amazement he added urgently, 'Only if you help me.'

'All right,' he said. 'We'll sing together. What shall we sing?'

'The two brooms,' Nico said.

Franco sat down on a bench with Nico standing between his knees. The accordionist struck up, and Franco began to sing in his pleasant, light baritone. After one short verse, Nico took over. The song was about two brooms having an argument.

'The mistress wrote this for them,' Celia said in an undervoice.

'Yes, I guessed that,' Joanne said with a smile. 'It's her style.'

She could hear Rosemary's voice through the comic words, as the brooms squabbled about which one cleaned the best. The song ended on a yell, but then the two singers hugged each other. It was a real hug, arms wide and tightly enveloping.

Two against the world, Joanne thought wistfully. They don't really need me.

An impromptu dance followed. Franco did a series of duty dances before approaching Joanne. 'Will you dance with me?' he asked.

'I think I should help Celia with the washing-up,' she said hastily.

For answer he held out his hand. His eyes were fixed on her face, demanding that she yield. She was swept by temptation. It would be sweet to dance with him, feeling him hold her close. And surely she could allow herself this one indulgence?

But there were some pleasures that were not for her. She would leave first thing next day, and forget this enchanted interlude. She backed away from him, smiling but firm. 'It's better if we don't,' she said.

'Are you angry with me, Joanne?'

'No, I'm not angry. But I don't really belong here.'

'How can you say that? Who belongs here more than you?'

'I don't think so. The sooner I leave the better.'

He laid his hand on her arm. His touch seemed to burn her. 'Do you think I'll let you just disappear?'

She couldn't answer, he affected her so powerfully. She'd tried to resist, but he would not be resisted. He took one of her hands in his and drew her into the shadows. 'They won't miss us for a while,' he said.

He led her on through the trees, until they reached a clearing on the far side. The valley stretched out before them, almost in darkness, for the moon was hidden behind clouds. But at that moment the clouds parted and the scene was flooded with brilliant silver moonlight. They stood watching it for a moment, awed by its ghostly beauty.

'The light appears like that,' Franco said at last. 'Suddenly, when you least expect it, driving away the darkness. And then you understand that this was why you clung on when all hope seemed to be gone. Because one day this moment would come.'

She couldn't speak for the beating of her heart. His words seemed to promise so much, if only she dared believe them...

'Dance with me,' he said again.

She could no longer resist what her heart longed for. She went easily into his arms and felt him draw her close. The party was so far away that even the lights were hidden by the trees, but they could still hear the sweet wail of an accordion, playing the yearning notes of a waltz.

He moved her gently this way and that, swaying to the time of the music. She followed his lead, feeling the warmth of his body against hers, the movements of his limbs. They danced as one, lost in the same dream, or so it seemed to her. They might have been alone on a distant planet, the first man and woman, existing before time began, dancing to the music of the spheres. She longed for it to last for ever.

But she knew that nothing so sweet ever lasted. She must cherish the precious moment, for it might be all she ever had.

'Joanne,' he said softly, 'look at me.'

She looked up and found his mouth very close. His eyes held hers for a moment, before he tightened his arms and touched her lips with his own.

She felt herself flower into life under the kiss she'd longed for. This was the man she loved, no matter how hard she tried not to. She'd fought her feelings for years, but he was her destiny, and she was in his arms, feeling his lips move softly over hers.

It was a kiss such as a young boy might have given, uncertain of his welcome, fearful to offend. But as he grew more sure of her his lips became ardent, purposeful, thrilling her with the intent she could feel. She pressed closer to him, eagerly seeking deeper caresses, and he responded by teasing her lips apart.

She was ready at that moment to yield him all of herself, heart, soul and body. She would give everything for one night of happiness and never count the cost. But in the same moment a little demon spoke in her head. It had Franco's voice and it said, You must hear, so that you may know never to trust me.

His warning had cast a shadow over every kiss, every gentle word. It ruined this moment which might have been so beautiful. The spell was broken and, try as she might, there was no way to bring it back now.

She could feel Franco's passion growing, his arms tightening about her. The ardour in his kisses made it hard to think but she knew she mustn't succumb. Putting out all her strength, she broke free.

'Joanne…'

'Please,' she begged. 'Let me go. We must stop this.'

'Why?' he demanded urgently.

'We have to get back. They'll notice we've gone.'

He let his hands fall, but she could still sense the trembling that shook him. 'Is that the only reason?' he asked raggedly.

'O-of course,' she stammered.

In a voice grown suddenly harsh he demanded, 'Are you sure it has nothing to do with Leo Moretto?'

For a moment she couldn't think whom he meant.

She was so caught up with the enchantment of being with him that no other man existed.

'What do you mean?' she asked.

Franco turned away from her as if wrenching himself by an effort. She saw him run both hands through his hair. His whole body radiated tension. At last he seemed to feel that it was safe to speak.

'I saw you together last night, saw how ardently you kissed him. I heard what he said, *"Carissima,* I adore you.'' He adores, but he doesn't know how to *love.* Loving a woman is when she gets under your skin so that you can't forget her however hard you try. It means watching her face to know what pleases her, what hurts her. It means lying awake, thinking of her in the arms of another man, wanting to—'

He stopped and drew a sharp breath. A rider who'd reined his horse back from the edge of a precipice might have made that sound.

'Franco, what is it?' she asked, not daring to believe that he was speaking of herself.

'Nothing! I only meant—you implied that I'd driven you into his arms,' he said awkwardly, 'and I didn't want that on my conscience.'

She longed to ask, 'Is that all it is?' But it was too much to hope that he might be jealous. Things were moving too fast, leaving her in a whirl. He raised his head to look at her and she saw in his eyes something that might have been her heart's desire. But then again she could be deceiving herself. His next words would tell her.

'Papa! Papa!'

The sound of Nico's voice seemed to fall between them. Whatever Franco had been going to say, he wouldn't say it now. She saw the shock on his face as he returned to the real world, and guessed that it mirrored her own. She forced herself to turn to where Nico was running through the trees.

'Papa, people are getting ready to go,' he cried. 'Everyone wonders where you are.' He looked innocently from one to the other.

Joanne recovered first. 'Your papa was showing me the view of the valley,' she said. 'It's very beautiful.'

Franco spoke up before Nico could ask any questions. 'But we should go back now,' he said hastily. 'I should never have neglected our guests.'

'Zia?' Nico held out his hand to her.

'I'll stay here a little longer,' she said. Returning with Franco would be too obvious, and there must be enough knowing looks going around already.

She gave them a head start, then followed to where the party was coming to an end. She managed to slip into the kitchen without being noticed. Celia was there, washing up, and Joanne picked up a towel. To her relief Celia asked no questions.

From outside Joanne could make out Franco's voice, raised in farewell, the sound of car doors slamming. Soon it was quiet. Nico ran in, followed by Franco, and gave Celia a smacking kiss. 'Thank you for my party,' he said.

He kissed Joanne too and said, 'Are you coming up with me?'

'I think it should be just your papa tonight.'

'Come, Nico,' Franco called. 'Whoah! Don't choke me. Come away to bed with you!'

'You go with them,' Celia urged.

'No,' Joanne said stubbornly. 'I'll stay here and help you.'

Celia fell silent. There was no arguing with the look on Joanne's face.

When everything was done Celia looked around. 'Where are those puppies?'

'They went into the garden a few minutes ago,' Joanne said. 'You go to bed. I'll find them.'

Celia departed and Joanne wandered outside. The coloured lamps were still on, casting a magic glow over the house and the garden.

'Pepe,' she called softly. 'Zaza.'

She heard a faint rustle in the bushes and went to investigate. Two bright eyes gleamed at her through a shock of hair.

'Zaza, there you are. Come on, it's time for bed.'

She picked up the furry bundle and looked around. 'Pepe, where are you?'

'I have her here,' came Franco's voice.

She made her way back to where he was standing with Pepe tucked under his arm. He took Zaza from her, set both pups down and shooed them into the house.

'Don't run away,' he said. 'I have things to say. I promise not to touch you.'

He thrust his hands in his pockets and headed away under the trees, the lamps throwing their lights on his black hair. Joanne followed, keeping a few paces away, not allowing herself to catch up when he stopped and leaned against a tree. He seemed to be having trouble finding the words.

'You're upset with me,' he said at last. 'And I can't blame you. I had no right to kiss you. I don't know what came over me. I apologise.'

'You don't need to apologise,' she said, trying to muffle her disappointment.

'But I do. My only excuse is that, after all this time, I'm still a little crazy.'

Joanne went closer to him, moved by the bleakness in his voice. She'd resolved to put a distance between them, to keep herself safe. But now her own safety counted for nothing, and all she cared about was to comfort him. If only she knew the way.

'I walk and talk like a normal man,' Franco said, 'but inside here—' he touched his breast '—there is still confusion, words that I can't speak, thoughts that I'm afraid of.'

Joanne put out her hand and found it clasped fiercely in his.

'You don't need to tell me about those thoughts,' she said. 'You've already warned me about them. I can cope.'

'You're very generous with my selfishness,' he said with a faint touch of bitterness.

'Franco, I—' Joanne stopped, amazed by the idea that had come to her, and by the strength of the impulse to put it into words. They didn't seem to be her own words. She wasn't sure where they'd come from, but the need to say them was overwhelming.

'I think there has to be a place for you where the sadness ends, and life is worth living again,' she began hesitantly. 'And perhaps I can be the bridge to that place. It troubles you to look at me because I'm half Rosemary and half not. If the half that's her can be any help to you, then—then use it. And when you reach the other side of the bridge, you'll be safe.'

'And you?' he asked, looking at her curiously. 'What about you when I've made use of you like this?'

'Well, that's the idea of bridges. You leave them

behind. I'm not suggesting anything that I can't cope
with.'

'And where does Leo Moretto come in all this?'

She was about to say that he came nowhere, when
it occurred to her that if Franco thought she had another
man to turn to in the end he would find her offer easier
to accept.

'Leo's my problem,' she said. 'He knows where he
stands with me, and I know where I stand with him.'

'And where exactly is that?'

'It doesn't matter.'

'Meaning, mind my own business? In that case, I
might ask why you kissed me back there, but I know
the answer. You were always a very kind person.'

Before she could speak they heard the sound of a
car approaching.

'Who can be arriving at this hour?' Franco mused.
'*Damn!* Talk of the devil!'

Leo came to a sharp halt and hopped out of the car.
'*Ciao,* Franco,' he called, waving cheerily. '*Ciao,*
Joanne.'

'What a surprise,' Franco said in a tight voice. 'Was
I expecting you?'

'You should have known that I wouldn't miss Nico's
birthday. I came to bring his present.'

He held up a parcel, tied up in brown paper.

'That's very kind of you,' Franco said politely. 'I'm
afraid my son's in bed.'

'No, I'm not,' came Nico's voice from overhead.
'Hallo, Uncle Leo.'

'All right, you can come down,' Franco said in a
resigned voice in which Joanne could detect an under-
tone of anger. But the anger was for Leo, not his son.

Nico's head vanished from the window, and he appeared in pyjamas a moment later.

Leo's gift was a jigsaw puzzle. He helped Nico unpack it onto the table under the trees.

'Now he expects me to invite him to supper,' Franco growled, drawing her aside.

'Well, why shouldn't you? He's an old friend. Stop scowling.'

For answer, Franco scowled at her too.

Leo and Nico had their heads together over the jigsaw, laughing. Celia was putting food on the table.

'When I saw Signor Leo arrive I knew he would want to eat,' she explained.

'I'm at home wherever I go,' Leo explained merrily. As if oblivious to the atmosphere, he tucked in.

'Have you had a good day?' he asked Joanne, blowing her a kiss.

'Yes, thank you. We've all enjoyed Nico's birthday very much.'

'Good. I'll drive you back to Turin tomorrow if you like.'

'It's very kind of you,' Franco said politely, 'but I can take Joanne myself, when she's ready to go.'

'But I've got to go there tomorrow anyway. Why not come with me?'

'Joanne's employers gave her permission to be away as long as she wished,' Franco said. 'You heard them.'

Laughing, Leo rose from the table and seized Joanne's hand in his. 'Wait till you hear what I've got planned,' he teased. 'I know a lovely little restaurant in Asti, very intimate—'

'Where you take all your conquests,' Franco said coldly.

'Ah, but Joanne isn't a conquest. She's making me

work to win her, aren't you, *mi amore?* Tomorrow I shall buy you the best food and wine in Piedmont, and afterwards I know a little spot where—'

'I'm afraid your plans will have to wait,' Franco interrupted him. 'Nico and I will be going to Lake Garda for a week—and Joanne is coming with us.'

CHAPTER EIGHT

FOR two days after Franco's surprise announcement
Isola Magia was abuzz with preparations. Celia set herself to launder practically every garment in the place,
despite Franco's insistence that they would need very
little.

His own time was taken up giving instructions to his
foreman. Joanne spent hours shopping for clothes in
Asti. The overnight bag Maria had packed for her contained only the basics. There wasn't enough there for
a vacation, and Joanne was determined not to wear
anything of Rosemary's.

She agonized for ages over suitable swimwear, un-
able to choose between a bikini or a sleek one-piece.
She'd been invited mainly for Nico's benefit, which
meant the one-piece. But then she remembered how her
invitation had come about. She would have sworn that
Franco had had no such intention a moment before. It
had been said to drive Leo off. When she thought of
something that had flashed in his eyes as he'd spoken,
she felt that a bikini might be the right choice after all.

But perhaps she was reading too much into that look.
Maybe she'd only imagined the enchanted dream when
they'd danced in the moonlight. She bought the one-
piece.

She returned to Isola Magia laden down with parcels,
but with spirits buoyed up at the prospect of a week at
Lake Garda, close to Franco.

As she entered the house she could hear the telephone ringing. There was no sign of anyone about, so she answered it.

'So you are there,' said a sour voice.

'Sophia?'

'I still have friends there, and they tell me what is happening,' said Franco's mother. 'I heard that you'd returned.'

Her tone was unpleasant, but Joanne remained determinedly courteous. 'I'm working in Italy now, quite near here. Naturally I came to see Rosemary's husband and child.'

'And to see if you could take up where you left off?'

'If that's what the gossips are telling you, they're wrong,' Joanne said firmly. 'I'm here mainly for Nico's sake. Yesterday was his birthday—'

'Don't tell me my own grandson's birthday.'

'I was only trying to explain that Franco felt—since Nico knows me—'

'It's just because you look like her. Oh, yes, I know all about that. "Rosemary came back to life." That's what they say. Franco's using you. Have you no pride?'

Joanne drew a slow breath and chose her words carefully. 'I don't think my pride matters. I'm needed. I'll help in any way I can.'

Sophia's voice hovered on the edge of a sneer. 'And that's why you're going to Lake Garda with them? To help?'

'That's right.'

'Well, my dear, I very much admire you.' The silky words made Joanne apprehensive as the open rudeness had failed to do. 'You know, of course, that the villa is where they spent their honeymoon?'

'I don't—see that makes any difference,' Joanne said

resolutely. The news made her heart sink, but she strove not to reveal how much she minded.

'Of course not. They rented it the first time, but their honeymoon was so happy that Franco bought it for her. They went back every year to rediscover their happiness. He really didn't tell you that?'

'Why should Franco tell me? It's none of my business.' To her relief she saw Franco entering. 'He's here now. Goodbye.'

She handed him the phone and escaped.

Their honeymoon villa! Why should he tell her? She'd assured herself that none of this mattered as long as she could give them what they needed. But it shocked her to discover how much she minded.

Celia had just returned from buying food. Joanne went to help her unpack the shopping in the kitchen. Franco's voice could be heard faintly, speaking in a placating tone.

'The Signora?' Celia said in a half-whisper.

Joanne nodded. 'I answered the phone. She wasn't pleased to find me here, or about me going to the lake with them.'

'She's not pleased, ever,' Celia said with a snort. 'When the mistress die she come here and take over. Order me out of the kitchen. Everything must be done her way, until Signor Franco said she should let me get on with my work. Then she make a big scene.

'She try to change Nico's life. Everything his mother did was wrong, she say. He's just a little boy. He's lost his mama. His father's going about in a daze, and suddenly this woman is trying to turn him against his mama.'

'That's inexcusable,' Joanne said.

'*Sì*. Is an *infamia*. So Signor Franco say no, she must

not do this. Another big scene. And we're all hoping she go back to her own home, but she stay and she stay and she stay. I think she stay for ever, but then her husband come here and say she must go back to Naples with him.

'Signor Franco try to keep the peace. He respect his mother. Also he love her, but she don't wanna believe that. She think—if you love her, you gotta do everything she say. If you don't, is not love.'

Joanne nodded. 'People like that are very frightening, because their minds are closed.'

'*Sì!* So now, she hear about you, and she get mad, because she think Signor Franco marry you, and she don't like that. Everyone else like it, though.'

'Celia, please, don't talk like that,' Joanne said urgently. 'I'm only here to help Nico.'

'Yeah, sure!' Celia said, lapsing in slang in her disconcerting way.

Joanne wandered out of the house, sunk in thought. She remembered Rosemary saying that Sophia had hated her, and she had no doubt that it was true. Franco was her darling, and she'd never forgiven the woman who'd won his heart. Now it seemed that resentment had been transferred to herself.

She found Nico and joined in a romp with Pepe and Zaza, but they only had half her attention. The other half was wondering when Franco would come off the phone.

He was away for a long time, and when he appeared he wore an expression of displeasure that told its own story.

'Go and give those pups a bath,' he commanded, tweaking Nico's hair. 'Otherwise we won't take them with us.'

'Papa, you promised!'

'Go and clean them up, then.'

When Nico had raced away, his two boon companions lolloping at his heels, Franco said, 'What did you mean when you told my mother that it was "none of your business"?'

'She asked if you'd told me about your honeymoon at Lake Garda,' Joanne said lightly. 'But why should you?'

Franco ran a hand distractedly through his hair. 'That's why I originally refused to go. I should have told you—'

'But why?' she asked with a cheerful shrug. 'We're doing this for Nico. How can the details matter?'

Franco frowned, uncertain how to read her tone. But Joanne had anticipated this, and she'd had enough time to get her reaction precisely right. As she'd intended, her smile and her manner gave nothing away.

'My mother—' he began '—she means well, and she wants only the best for me.'

'I'm sure she does, like all mothers,' Joanne said brightly. 'Now, perhaps I should go and help Nico bath those dogs.'

Nothing more was said on the subject, and the preparations continued. Joanne lovingly unwrapped her new clothes and packed them away in a suitcase. The sight of them made her feel better.

She wondered what had been said between Franco and his mother, but he never mentioned it, and by the next morning they were ready to leave. Nico and the puppies piled into the car, Franco stowed the last of the baggage aboard, and they were off.

'It's about two hundred miles,' Franco said. 'We should be there by late afternoon.'

It was an enchanted journey, through the most beautiful scenery she'd ever seen. Had there ever been such a fertile country? she thought as they travelled past silvery olive groves, beneath palm trees and cypress. In the distance she could see mountains, covered in snow that looked almost blue, although down here the summer heat was growing fierce.

Franco drove with the windows down, one arm resting on the edge, the other hand controlling the wheel with light movements. Joanne was glad to see that he looked relaxed.

She spent the first part of the journey sitting beside him while Nico sat in the back explaining everything to Pepe and Zaza. They stopped for a coffee, and when they resumed the journey Joanne sat in the back and chatted to Nico. He was eager to tell her about where they were going.

'It's in a little fishing village called Peschino, and the villa is right at the edge of the lake, so we can run out onto the beach and into the water. And all the fishermen are our friends, especially the Terrinis, who live near. There are lots and lots of them. And the house is called the Villa Felicità.'

'The Villa of Happiness.' Joanne tried the words.

'It used to be called something else, but Mama and Papa were so happy there that they renamed it,' Nico said innocently, unaware that he was turning a knife in her breast.

Joanne heard Franco take a sharp breath, and spoke quickly. 'Those hills are so beautiful, as if they were covered in gold.'

'Those are orange and lemon groves,' Nico said. 'And over there—look, *Zia*—'

He prattled on happily and the dangerous moment passed.

Joanne's first impression of Lake Garda was of flowers. Camellias, azaleas, rhododendrons, geraniums everywhere, spilling over the banks, their brilliant colours rioting in the sun.

To get to Peschino they had to drive right around to the west shore, so the last part of the journey was spent with the lake in view. She drank in its beauty, the impossible blue of the water, the red-tiled villas that nestled against the hills, flanked by fruit and olives.

'We're nearly there,' Franco told them as he drove into the little town of Bardolino. 'Shall we stop for a coffee?'

Joanne was about to say that she'd love one when she realized that Nico was crossing his fingers.

'Do you want to?' he asked her politely.

'I think we should just get straight on,' she said, ruffling his hair.

'Yes, *please*,' he cried in relief, and Franco shouted with laughter.

'You said the right thing,' he told her.

'I remember when I was a child, and we were going to the seaside, and when we were on the last lap some wretched adult always wanted to stop and make you wait for the treat,' she said.

Nico nodded vigorously, pleased at her understanding.

Half an hour later they reached Peschino, a tiny place out of a picture book that Joanne loved on sight: the roads that ran down straight onto the sand, the little fishing boats bobbing on the water, the cafés with their tables and chairs outside, the tiny population who all seemed to know each other. Franco told her that this was literally true.

'There aren't more than eight hundred people here and over the years they've intermarried. Somehow everyone is related to everyone else. Weddings, funerals and baptisms are great occasions.'

The villa was an enchanted place, with cool *terrazzo* floors and huge windows. Gina Terrini, who cared for it in Franco's absence, came, smiling, to welcome them. She was a plump, middle-aged woman, who hugged Nico and greeted Franco as an old friend. Her eyes briefly flickered over Joanne, but she showed no surprise. She'd put her and Franco in separate rooms, and Joanne guessed that he'd briefed her well.

Joanne's room had a tall window that overlooked the garden, and then the lake. It was dark from the closed shutters, but she pushed them open and breathed in the fresh, glorious air. When she'd unpacked she went to find the others, and found them in the kitchen, seated around the table gossiping nineteen to the dozen. Nico was drinking milk and munching almond biscuits. Gina and Franco were drinking *prosecco,* and she immediately set one in front of Joanne.

'Now I go,' she declared. 'But tonight, you come to us for supper.'

'Gina comes from the family Nico was telling you about,' Franco explained. There are plenty of them, including five children.'

'Six,' Gina said at once. 'Since last year. And my brother's wife is pregnant.'

'Which brother?' Nico asked.

Gina shrugged. 'One of them.'

'That little house is going to burst with all of you,' Franco protested.

'Oh, no, we've got the house next door now, so we can stay together.'

Nico clamoured to be allowed to go with Gina and meet his friends again.

'You do your unpacking first,' Franco told him. 'And put everything away tidily. Don't leave it all to Joanne.'

Nico seized Joanne's hand, putting his whole heart into the one word, *'Please.'*

'Nico, what did I say?' Franco asked firmly.

'I take good care of him,' Gina put in.

'Let him go,' Joanne begged. 'Let him enjoy himself.'

'OK, I'm outvoted,' Franco said with humorous resignation.

Nico's shriek of joy made them all cover their ears. The next moment he was out of the door, bounding along the beach with the pups gambolling beside him, and Gina trying to keep up.

'Thank you,' Franco said. 'He's happy now. Do you think you can be happy here for a week?'

'I think it's the loveliest place I've ever seen. And you? How will you manage?'

'It's time I laid my ghosts. And I'm in good company.'

She wasn't quite sure what he meant by that, and he didn't explain.

'I should tell you some more about the Terrini family, because you'll probably find them a little overwhelming. There's Papa and Mama Terrini, their two sons, and Gina, their daughter, their sons' wives, a couple of teenage boys, and lots of children.'

'I should think they do need the house next door,' Joanne said. 'Why must they all stay together?'

'Italians believe families belong together. Besides, the men are all fishermen. It's a family business, and it's more convenient to live beside the boats.'

He carried their cases upstairs and Joanne did her own unpacking, then Nico's. On her way back from his room she passed the open door of Franco's room. The sight of him struggling to keep things in order took her back over the years and she stopped to watch. Her chuckle made him look up and he grinned ruefully.

'Let me do it,' she said, coming inside. 'You always were the most untidy man in the world.'

'Only for some things,' he defended himself. 'I keep the estate books in perfect order.'

'Yes, but get you inside a house and things just seem to rearrange themselves into a mess,' she said, taking clothes out of his case and hanging them up. 'I remember your mother saying that.'

'And I remember her telling me to get my room tidy in half an hour, and you doing it for me. I took you out to a meal as a thank you, didn't I?'

'No, you were going to, but you forgot,' she said lightly. 'Where do you want this shirt?'

'Anywhere will do.'

'That's the attitude that got you into a mess in the first place,' she told him severely. He grinned with a touch of sheepishness, just like the old days. And her heart did somersaults. Just like the old days.

When she'd finished he took her out to show her the village. Peschino was little more than five streets, converging around a bustling market. There were a few tourists' shops and cafés, but it was still mostly a working fishing port.

He'd told her that it was like a huge family, and wherever they went they were pursued by cries of,

'Franco! *Hey, Franco!*' People remembered him and called him from doors and windows, running out to shake his hand and exult.

There was one awkward moment when a man cried, 'And Signora Rosemary. We heard a rumour you were dead. How nice to see you alive and well.'

Appalled, Franco explained, the man made hasty apologies and faded away. They looked awkwardly at each other.

'I'm sorry, Joanne.'

'Will you buy me a cup of coffee?' Joanne asked. 'We should talk.'

They settled at a table outside Luigi's, a small café where the owner greeted him lustily. When their coffee had been served, Joanne said, 'We've got to face this ghost and stop running away from it.'

'I had no right to impose such burdens on you,' he said heavily.

'You let me worry about that,' she replied briskly. 'I knew what I was doing when I took this on, and I'm not going to collapse like a wilting violet every time someone calls me Rosemary. Anyway, nobody will, now. After what just happened, it will be all around the village.'

'True.'

'Nico's got it clear in his head,' Joanne said. 'And I've sorted myself out about it.'

It was a lie. Her ghost was the thought of their honeymoon. But she was determined to banish that one too.

'You're the one who's still troubled,' she said. 'I'm afraid it will be harder on you than anyone.'

After a moment he said, 'At first I looked at you and saw her, and there was a cruel moment when I faced the truth all over again. Not any more. Now I see you. Your voice is different, and you say things she would never have said. And I'm glad to be here with you.'

Because he'd said that, the sun was brighter, the air more clear and pure. But all she said was, 'That's what I meant about being your bridge. Now, come along, we're all going to enjoy ourselves.'

They returned to the house to shower and dress. She put on a bright blue linen dress and brushed out her hair, letting it fall naturally about her shoulders. Franco wore jeans and a white shirt, open at the throat. He'd meant to visit a barber before they'd left, but there hadn't been time, and now his hair curled about his collar and fell over his forehead. It made him young again, less severe, and ten times as attractive.

When it was time for supper they went the few yards along the beach and were engulfed in the family. Franco introduced her to everyone but she soon lost track of husbands, wives, children in a tidal wave of hospitality.

But then she discovered a snag. This side of the lake belonged to the Veneto region, and Joanne, whose ears were just becoming used to Piedmontese, found herself among people who didn't use it. *La madre lingua*, as Italian was known, was useful for watching television and dealing with officials, but at home civilized folk spoke Venetian.

At first she was sure she'd never fit in, but with these cheerful people being a wallflower just wasn't an option. Between two languages, a dialect and a lot of laughter, they all found a way to understand each other.

The problems of living in two houses had been solved very simply. The fences between the front and back gardens had been removed, and it seemed as if no doors were ever closed. Folk wandered in and out as they pleased, and soon Joanne stopped trying to work out who lived where, who was called what, who was married to whom, or who was whose offspring. After all, what did it matter?

She even found herself giving the characteristic Italian shrug with its implications of not worrying about trifles. She was with the man she loved, in a closeness that would once have seemed an impossible dream. All else was a trifle.

Supper was mussel soup followed by fillet steaks with brandy and Marsala, cooked in the first kitchen. This was followed by caramel oranges and *asiago,* a mountain cheese from the region, both prepared in the second kitchen. Joanne found that all her hosts and hostesses wanted a share of her, and she went back and forth between kitchens, slicing garlic in one, and adding kirsch to syrup in the other, struggling to understand and make herself understood, and laughing a lot.

The meal was served outside on two small tables pushed together to make one large one, so that everyone could see everyone else's face, and all shout together. Papa Terrini produced bottles from an apparently inexhaustible supply of Raboso and Soave, clapped Franco on the shoulder, kissed Joanne's hand and yelled, 'Eat! Eat!'

Italy was a country of plenty, and never more so than when entertaining guests. The Terrinis were poor but they ate and drank with gusto, laughed and loved with vigour and took no thought for the morrow. Joanne, who spent too much time worrying about the morrow, found her cares slipping away from her in a riot of colour, wine and pleasure.

Best of all, Franco seemed affected the same way.

From across the table he raised his glass to her. She saluted him back, drained her glass, and immediately found it filled again by Tonio or Plinio or Marco or whoever...

They strolled home in the moonlight, Nico between them, too sleepy to talk. When they'd put him to bed Joanne yawned. 'I'm not used to all this riotous living,' she murmured. 'I can hardly keep my eyes open.'

'It was a very long journey,' Franco said. 'And the wine was very potent.'

'And very plentiful,' she added with a slight chuckle. 'I really drank more of it than I should.'

'You certainly are a trifle flushed,' Franco agreed, considering her face and smiling. 'The sooner you go to bed the better.'

He escorted her to her door, and opened it for her. 'You can sleep late tomorrow, if you wish. Goodnight, Joanne.'

She fully expected to take advantage of his offer, but the air of the lake was stimulating, and she awoke early, feeling fresh and ready to enjoy herself. There'd been a hint of admiration in Franco's eyes when he'd smiled at her last night, and something in his voice as he'd said her name—

She told herself to stop this. She was building on nothing. But she could no more prevent herself examining every look and word for hope than lovers had ever been able to do.

Over breakfast the others were full of plans to take a boat trip one of Gina's brothers had offered them. Joanne hastily declined.

'I'm not good in boats. I get queasy very easily. You two go.'

'But you must come,' Nico protested.

'Not if it's really going to make you feel bad,' Franco said. 'But we can't go off and abandon you.'

'Nonsense, I shall have a wonderful time exploring. There are some ruins near here. Someone told me about them last night—'

'But you can't remember who,' Franco said wickedly.

'No, I can't. But I do remember about the ruins. I shall take my sketch-pad, and have a fine time.'

She resisted all attempts to persuade her. She felt that father and son should have some time together without her, and she really was unhappy in a boat. When Franco saw that she meant what she said he gave her his car keys, bid her enjoy herself, and followed Nico out to the beach.

She did enjoy herself, roaming the picturesque ruins, making sketch after sketch, and finally driving back in the late afternoon.

She stopped in the village to buy some sun cream, and dawdled, looking at the shops. Suddenly the tasteful clothes she'd bought for this trip seemed a waste of money. She wanted something colourful and crazy; the crazier the better. She found a shop selling beach wear and beach equipment, and purchased a gaily coloured, wide skirt and matching scarf. Then, in a moment of madness, she chose a bikini. As bikinis went it was rather modest, but buying it felt like an act of liberation.

She almost danced out of the shop and immediately collided with someone coming in.

'I'm sorry,' said a young male voice. 'I was just about to catch your attention.'

'Leo!'

CHAPTER NINE

'LEO!' Joanne repeated. 'What are you doing here?'

'You don't say that as if you were delighted to see me,' he said sadly. 'Startled, yes. But not delighted. Let me buy you a coffee.'

They went to Luigi's and sat outside. Leo ordered coffee for them both. 'I was about to go and knock on your door,' he said. 'What luck to run into you when Franco isn't there looking daggers at me.'

'What are you doing here, Leo?' she asked wryly. She was becoming suspicious of him.

'What do you think I'm doing?'

'I think you've come to make mischief.'

He grinned sheepishly. 'Well—I'll admit I enjoy doing that. Come on, aren't you a little glad to see a man who adores you?'

His words made her face the fact that she wasn't glad at all. In fact she was rather annoyed with him for threatening to spoil this magic time.

'Of course you are,' he persisted. 'Maybe not very glad, since you're idiotically hung up about Franco. But a little bit.' His manner was teasing but confident, like a small boy who knew he could get away with anything.

'Not even a little bit,' she told him.

'You could be very depressing for a man without a lot of self-confidence,' he complained.

'What would you know about lacking confidence?' she asked with a reluctant smile.

'Let's put it this way. If you said you didn't like me at all, I wouldn't believe you. Because I still remember that smoochy kiss you gave me in the Antoninis' house that night. If Franco hadn't turned up—who knows?'

'I did like you a little,' Joanne said wryly. 'You reminded me strongly of someone, although I couldn't think who. Since then it's come to me.'

'Aha! That's better! Who do I remind you of? Mel Gibson? Warren Beatty?'

'Franco. As he was, years ago.'

For once Leo was really taken aback. He opened and closed his mouth, and let out a long breath.

'Well, I guess he's done it again,' he said at last.

'Done what?'

'Years ago he balked me in the *palio*. Now it's the same story. I just can't win against him.'

'It depends what you're trying to win. You don't really want me. You're just playing games.'

'And you don't want to play games with me?'

'No, I don't.'

'So you won't have dinner with me tonight?'

'No, but I'll invite you home to dinner with Franco and Nico and me.'

He made a face. 'Thank you, but I'll decline that charming invitation. I've just about time to drive home. There's nothing to keep me here, is there?'

'No,' she said firmly. 'There isn't. Goodbye, Leo.'

On the way home she debated whether to tell Franco about Leo's visit, but decided not to. He might read the wrong thing into it.

She found the others already there. It had obviously been a tiring day, for they didn't have much to say about what they'd done. Franco seemed a little distracted, and refused Gina's invitation to come over for dinner.

'Thank you, but not tonight,' he said with a brief smile. 'We'll eat out.'

They found a little *trattoria* and ate pasta and fish soup. Joanne was puzzled. A malaise that she couldn't explain seemed to have fallen over them. They were all glad when the evening was over.

Last night she'd slept like a log. Tonight she was restless, tossing until two in the morning. At last she got up, threw on a robe meaning to go downstairs.

But once in the corridor she heard her own name spoken and stopped. The sound was coming from Nico's room. Through the open door Joanne could see Franco sitting on the bed, listening to Nico who was talking earnestly.

'But why didn't Aunt Joanne just tell us she wanted to see Uncle Leo, Papa? Why pretend she didn't like boats?'

'Perhaps she thought we wouldn't like her seeing Uncle Leo.'

'Does Aunt Joanne like Uncle Leo better than she likes you?'

'Maybe. She likes us differently. We don't own her, you know.'

'But aren't you going to marry Aunt Joanne?'

She'd been about to push open the door, tell them what she'd heard, and set right the misunderstanding. But at this question Joanne stopped, frozen.

The silence seemed to go on for ever before Franco said, 'I don't know.'

'Wouldn't it would be lovely if you did?' Nico said wistfully.

'Yes, it would be lovely,' Franco agreed in what sounded to Joanne like an awkward voice.

'Couldn't you make Uncle Leo go away?'

'Suppose he won't go?'

'He will if you tell him Aunt Joanne likes you best.'

Silence. Then Franco's voice, sounding rather heavy. 'That's enough for tonight, my son.'

Joanne backed away. She'd heard too much and too little. Enough to know that Franco knew of her meeting with Leo and thought she'd arranged it. Enough to know that he minded. But not enough to know why he minded, or how he really felt about her. She wanted to laugh and cry.

Franco tucked his son up, kissed him, and went to the door. He stood there a long time, watching the sleeping child. As he stepped out into the corridor he paused, wondering if he'd really heard a sound. But the corridor was empty, and the house was silent.

At breakfast next morning Joanne took the first chance to say casually, 'By the way, Leo was here yesterday. I bumped into him in town, and we had a coffee.'

'Why did he have to come?' Nico asked in a rebellious voice. 'We don't want him.'

'Nico, that's very rude,' Franco reproved. But he spoke without heat, as if he secretly agreed with his son.

'Well, he's gone again, so we don't have to have him,' Joanne said cheerfully. 'He was only passing through.'

'Are you sure he won't come back?' Nico demanded.

'If he does I'll tell him we don't want him,' Joanne promised.

Nico looked happier, and Joanne was relieved. The worst thing would be to have the child thinking she'd deceived them to meet Leo secretly. Franco gave her a grin, as though he too was free of a load, and she suddenly found that she was having trouble breathing.

It was absurd to be acting like a fluttery teenager after all this time. But the man she loved had smiled at her with meaning, and she wanted to sing for joy.

'Can we go to the beach?' Nico demanded.

'We can do whatever you like,' Franco told him fondly. 'The beach it is.'

In her own room Joanne had a final dither between the one-piece and the bikini. At last she took a deep breath and put on the bikini, slipping the gaily coloured skirt over it.

The other two were waiting for her impatiently downstairs. 'Nico says if you don't hurry the water will have gone away,' Franco assured her. The three of them went out in high spirits.

They were spotted at once by the Terrini family, who joined them boisterously. Nico went off to play with the children, while two of the Terrini sons, both in their mid-teens, settled down to admire Joanne.

Yesterday they'd treated her with distant respect, as befitted the wife of an older man. But they'd obviously discovered that she and Franco weren't married, plus Gina had probably gossiped about the separate rooms. Now they felt free to throw themselves at her feet.

When she tossed aside the skirt for a swim they whistled in admiration, and jostled each other to keep near her in the water. Afterwards, as they all had a snack, the boys rushed to anticipate her every wish, doing antics trying to make her laugh, squabbling with each other for the privilege of sitting beside her. They were like innocent puppies, and she was entertained.

But later the fun got out of hand when they announced their intention of going out in the little dinghy, and taking her with them.

'No way,' she said, trying to pass it off with a laugh. 'I'm nervous in boats.'

'But we will keep you safe,' they protested. 'You come with us.'

For a few minutes they squabbled, the boys demanding, Joanne protesting, until finally they seized her hands and began to pull her down the sand to the water's edge.

'No!' she cried, beginning to be alarmed.

'It's all right. We look after you.'

'Basta!' Franco's voice was like the crack of a whip. 'Let her go.'

The boys stared, amazed by his transformation from a cheerful companion to a man with alarming anger in his eyes. To underline his point Franco put his arm about Joanne's waist and pulled her firmly against him, snapping out something curt in Venetian. She couldn't make out the words, but the boys released her and backed off, looking shamefaced.

'Are you all right?' Franco asked, still holding her.

'Y-yes, I'm fine,' she stammered, hoping she didn't sound as breathless as she felt. The bikini didn't feel so modest now that her skin was pressed against his.

'They're only children,' he said. 'They mean no harm, but they don't know when the joke's over.'

'Yes, of course.'

He touched her face lightly. 'Are you sure you're all right? You still look a little upset.'

She wasn't upset, but her heart was thumping from

being held so close to him. How could he hold her like
this, half naked, in front of all the world, and stay so
calm?

Then she saw a little pulse beating at his throat, and
understood that he wasn't calm at all. Suddenly he
tightened his arm and laid his mouth on hers. It was
only for a moment, and he pulled away at once, laughing and slightly self-conscious.

'They won't trouble you again now,' he said softly.
'I've made the matter plain.'

'Is the matter plain to you?' she whispered back.

He drew a ragged breath. 'No, not at all. It grows
more confused every moment.'

He let her go and turned away quickly. Joanne was
left feeling as if her whole body was blushing while
the Terrini clan looked on, exchanging nods and smiles
of understanding.

There was no chance of a private moment with him
after that. The boys' mothers converged on her, full of
apologies for their sons' behaviour. To make them feel
better she went into the house for a coffee and a chat,
where they all laughed at their language difficulties and
had a good time. But she knew they were thinking of
the little scene on the beach, and regarding her curiously.

Without warning, Mama Terrini demanded to know
if she could do Italian cooking. And, when she said no,
insisted on teaching her the secrets of *linguini* with
walnuts. Joanne concentrated, and the other women
pronounced her first attempt excellent.

To her embarrassment, Mama Terrini trumpeted her
achievement as she served the linguini that evening.
Everyone cheered, pronounced it delicious, and toasted
her. It would have been delightful if she hadn't been

growing more self-conscious by the minute. It was so obvious that these good-hearted people had decided she was to be Franco's wife. But what was he thinking? He was swapping cheerful insults with Papa Terrini, and seemed oblivious.

She was relieved to be able to slip out of the spotlight after that, except for the awkward moment when the boys apologised, their eyes nervously on Franco. She told them to forget it, and they hightailed it out of the house.

Nobody would have dreamed, from the lateness of the hour, that this was a family who had to rise early to catch fish. The party went on and on, always picking up with a fresh batch of coffee or wine. Children fell asleep in the arms of their parents, aunts or uncles, or simply whoever happened to be nearest, for in this warm-hearted country everyone was at ease with children, and children belonged to everyone.

Joanne sat cuddling a little girl whose name she hadn't caught, until the child's mother lifted her gently out of Joanne's arms, with a whispered *grazie,* and bore her off to bed.

On her other side, Nico was leaning against her, dozing with a smile on his face. 'It's time he was in bed, too,' she said, gathering him up into her arms.

She bid the others goodnight in a whisper, and they responded likewise. Franco watched her with softened eyes as she carried his little son away, the child's head drooping against her shoulder. After a moment he realized that Papa Terrini was speaking to him.

'I'm sorry,' he said hastily.

'I only asked if you want some more wine.'

'No—yes—thank you.'

'Is that a yes or a no?' Papa asked patiently.

'Er—no, I think.'

'My friend, you're in a bad way.'

'Yes, I think I am,' Franco murmured. He forced himself to sound bright. 'I mean, thank you, I'll have another glass.'

Joanne set the little boy down on the bed and began pulling off his shirt and jeans. He helped her like someone moving in his sleep, and when she pulled the duvet over him he still hadn't opened his eyes.

But some part of his mind was still with her, for he clung onto her hand. So she sat down on the bed and waited. When his regular breathing told her that he was asleep Joanne gently released her hand. Leaning down, she kissed his forehead too gently to awaken him, and crept out of the room.

Gina was there in the kitchen, having followed her home. Joanne smiled at her and slipped out of the house. She badly needed a walk in the cool fresh air.

On the beach she kicked off her shoes and strolled at the water's edge, letting the peace of the lake wash over her. It was a blessed relief to be where she could hear only the lapping of the water, and the sweet sound of an accordion floating along the shore from Bardolino.

'Is he asleep?'

Startled, Joanne turned and found Franco sitting on an upturned dinghy. She hadn't known he was there.

'Nico? Yes, he didn't really wake up to get undressed.'

'He trusts you. I'm glad.'

He gave her a glance of invitation, and she went to sit beside him on the boat, leaning back a little to look at the stars. In this clear air they seemed almost impossibly brilliant, and she felt giddy at the beauty.

'Careful, don't lean back too far,' he said, supporting her shoulders with his arm.

She didn't move, enjoying the feeling of his nearness. At this moment she wasn't thinking about passion, only the sweetness of being here quietly together.

Further along the beach a young couple strolled hand in hand, totally absorbed in each other. The young man turned and rested his arms on the girl's shoulders, his forehead against hers. Smiling, she put her arms about him, and looked directly into his eyes. His lips moved.

'I wonder what he's saying,' Joanne mused.

'Te voja ben,' Franco said.

'What's that?'

'It's Venetian. It means, I wish you well.'

Joanne smiled. 'No, I think he's saying something a little more significant than that.'

'To a Venetian there is nothing more significant than that. It means, I love you.'

'Oh, I see.' She didn't know what else to say.

Franco gently removed his arm and sat with his hands clasped, staring across the water. He spoke without looking at her.

'And what about Leo, Joanne? Does he wish you well?'

'I told you, Leo was just passing through.'

'That story will do for Nico, not for me. He drove all this way for a purpose. Did you exchange the words of lovers? I have no right to ask, of course. But I'm asking anyway.'

His voice and his attitude gave nothing away, but she could sense his tension, and she wondered if his heart was beating as urgently as her own.

'You don't answer,' Franco said at last. 'Perhaps that *is* my answer. Will you be leaving with him soon?'

'Of course not. As though I'd just abandon Nico like that!'

'And me, Joanne?' he asked quietly.

'No, I wouldn't abandon you, either.'

'Did you tell Leo to go away and come back later?'

'No, I just told him to go away.'

He turned his head to look at her. 'Only that?'

'Only that. There never was anything in it.' She smiled. 'He's still mad at you for making him fall off in the *palio*.'

'I know. He always will be. We're friendly, but he keeps trying to find ways to upset me. And this time he managed it.' He took her hand in his. 'I mind. Maybe I have no right to, but I mind.'

'There's nothing to mind about, Franco. Truly.'

He didn't answer directly, but sat looking down at her hand clasped in his. 'I've found myself remembering things about you, from eight years ago. The way you nursed Ruffo for me. Once I had to be away, and you stayed up with him all night. You saved his life.'

'You saved him, getting him away from those louts.'

'That was only the start. You gave him love. I saw how he greeted you, after all this time. He remembers, you see. Just as I remember.'

He fell silent. Joanne had a strange feeling that Franco was half in and half out of a dream. How much of what he was saying was memory, and how much projection back from now? Whatever the answer, it was very sweet to sit here, holding his hand.

'What do you remember, Franco?'

'About you? Lots of things. The way you were always rushing around, full of eagerness, wanting to do everything at once. You were so young and untouched. All the possibilities of the world seemed to be there in you.

'And then sometimes I'd see such a strange look in your face, as though you had a secret that made you sad. Why was that?'

'I can't remember,' she said. 'Everything seemed so important at that age.'

'And then you grow up, and the same things aren't important?'

'Well—some of them are. Some of them even more important.'

He raised his eyebrows in query, but she backed off. It had gone as close to the truth as she dared, but she would go no further.

'We used to be able to talk, as friends, didn't we?' he asked.

She chuckled. 'Most of our conversations consisted of you making me promise not to tell your mother about something you'd done.'

He grinned. 'That's true.'

'But if you need a friend now, I'm here for you.'

'And is that all you'll be to me, Joanne?'

'I don't know,' she said softly. 'Let's wait and see.'

'How wise you are. At first I was reluctant to bring you to this place, where I was happy with her. I thought it wouldn't be fair to you, and I was afraid of the memories. But now the memories are all kindly ones. Tonight I feel peaceful for the first time in a year, as though the world were once more a good place, where I could find a home. And that's your doing.'

Still holding her hand, he rose and led her back to the house. They bid goodnight to Gina, and while Franco locked up Joanne slipped upstairs to look in on

Nico. He was sleeping soundly, still in the same position she'd left him. Franco came in behind her and they stood watching for a moment, before backing out silently.

At her door he stopped. 'Joanne,' he said softly. 'Joanne…'

His kiss was gentle, one hand cupping her face while he explored her mouth with slow, tentative movements. When he felt her sway against him he let his arms slide right around her, holding her close.

This wasn't like last time, when he'd kissed her with fierce urgency. Now she could feel his uncertainty, as if every step were a minefield. They were both uncertain, wondering what lay just ahead, but wanting to search out the way to each other.

'Am I crazy?' he whispered against her mouth.

'If you are, I'm crazy too.'

'I've wanted to kiss you all day—and yesterday— when I saw you with Leo I could have—'

'Hush, I've told you about that.'

'I warned you, I'm a jealous man. Now tell me I have no right to be jealous. Tell me that what you do is none of my business—if you can.'

It was hard to think of words while his lips were trailing a path of fire along her jaw. His words teased her, but his mouth teased her more. She drew a long, trembling breath.

'You have no *need* to be jealous,' she murmured with difficulty.

'I'm jealous of every man who looks at you. If I'd had my way I'd have knocked those boys' heads together.'

'But they're just children,' she said, reminding him of his own words.

'They looked at you with the eyes of men, and I wanted to carry you off out of their sight. All I care about now is you, and how good it feels to have you in my arms. Say it's the same with you.'

She answered him, not in words, but with her mouth and the movements of her hands. She was where she longed to be, and there was nothing but this man and her love for him. No talk now, no arguments, just the wondrous feel of him close to her, wanting her with all his being. And the glorious certainty that she could give him what he needed.

Quietly she pushed open her door and took his hand to lead him inside. The room was dark, save for the moonlight coming through the tall window. It was open, the long gauze curtains whispering in the soft breeze. Outside the lake lay still, gleaming under the moon like a scene from a beautiful, alien world. In here was all the world she would ever want.

Franco put both his arms right around her, imprisoning her own arms between them, holding her gently while he laid his cheek against her hair.

'Are you sure?' he whispered.

'I'm quite sure. Hush, don't ask questions.'

He cupped her face in his hands, regarding her with searching intensity. He kissed her, not on the mouth but on the forehead, then the eyes, so lightly that he was barely touching her, yet she felt every movement as a delight. At last he laid his lips on hers, enfolding her in his arms and kissing her as though he were laying claim to her. She gave herself up to him without reservation. She was his to claim if only he wanted her.

She was still dressed in the flowing skirt over the bikini. She felt his fingers moving on the straps, drawing them gently down, releasing the clasp behind. Her breasts were full from the strength of her desire, the nipples proud and peaked. She knew the sight and feel of them would tell him of her passion. She drew a trembling breath as he let his hands drift slowly down to cup the fullness.

His gentleness was a revelation. He caressed her as though she were breakable, or perhaps it was the spell being woven between them that he feared to break. He pulled off his shirt and drew her against his bare chest. The feeling was so good that she gasped.

Lost in sensation, she hardly knew when he released the fastening of her skirt and let it fall. He gently removed the rest of her clothes, and his own, and led her towards the bed, drawing her down beside him, then leaning back to look at her. Her body was slim and elegant, the waist tiny, the breasts firm and generous. She was glad of it for his sake, because she wanted to make him a perfect gift.

His own naked body was a delight to her. She'd seen him in shorts, and knew the broad torso and muscular thighs. But the promise in his lean, powerful hips made the blood rush to her face and warmth engulf her. She wanted him to make love to her now, but yet how sweet it was to lie here, letting him prepare her slowly and tenderly for the joy to come.

He seemed awed by her, and caressed her almost reverently. Wherever she felt his touch she came newly aware with sensations she'd dreamed of but never known before, and she gave herself up to them eagerly. He pressed his face between her breasts, loving her tenderly with his lips and tongue. She clasped her hands behind his head, arching against him, seeking deeper pleasure from his skilled hands and mouth. With every flickering movement she felt fire stream along her nerves, until she was one pulsing, throbbing centre of desire.

She'd feared her own inexperience, but the strength of her love dispelled all doubts and made everything come naturally with him. She knew when he was ready to come over her, and she was eager to welcome him. At the moment of their union she sensed, rather than saw, his shock as he discovered that she was a virgin, but then everything was lost in the fusion of sensation and emotion.

She was moving easily and naturally in his rhythm, letting him guide her forward. She moaned softly with pleasure, wanting more yet content to trust in him for what was to come. Looking up into his face, she saw his smile of reassurance, and answered it with one of her own. Her heart was in that smile. If her life was a desert after this, still she'd had her moment of joy.

Her lips moved but no sound came. The pleasure was spiralling upwards, carrying her with it. Her breath came rapidly as she felt herself caught up in a force beyond her control. When the explosion of pleasure came she felt his arms strong about her, holding her safe as they reached the peak and plunged down, far down in a swirling abyss.

But he was there still, keeping her safe as she trembled. She closed her eyes and clung to him, feeling ecstasy turn into contentment. She'd come home at last, and it was a wonderful place, as she had always known it would be.

CHAPTER TEN

WHEN Joanne awoke she lay for a while with her eyes closed. She was sure that when she opened them she would find herself alone. Franco would have left before the light came, pursuing whatever delusion was sustaining him.

But when she looked he was sitting by the window, clad in a towelling robe, gazing out over the lake. One arm rested on his raised knee, and his head was thrown back against the wall. He looked the picture of contentment.

She made no sound or movement, but something seemed to tell him that she was awake and he turned to smile at her. That smile eased her heart. It was without strain, almost happy.

'Good morning,' he said.

'Good morning,' she replied, smiling back at him.

He came towards the bed, holding out his hands. She took one of them in hers as he sat down beside her. Her flesh was still alive with the feelings of last night.

'You should have told me,' he said gently. 'I never dreamed that it was possible. You're so beautiful, so warm. How could I be the first man to discover it?'

'I've done so much travelling around,' she said quickly. 'There's been no time to get to know people.' She kept her voice light. 'Always another picture to copy on the next horizon.'

'Yes, your life has been full of imitations,' he said. 'But last night—was no imitation.'

146

She looked at him steadily. 'No?'

'There was only you in my arms, and in my heart. Believe it, Joanne. Surely your own heart knew that before I told you?'

'I think so. But perhaps—' she lay a hand over his lips '—perhaps it doesn't matter right now.'

'You're right.' He leaned down to kiss her. 'Some things are too fragile to be talked about. But we must talk—some time.'

'Yes, some time,' she agreed. 'But not yet.'

At breakfast Nico was loud in his pleas to go swimming again. Franco agreed, but added, 'Not here, where we'll be overrun with Terrinis.'

They drove along the shore as far as Bardolino. Here the beach was more geared to tourists, with loungers and ice-cream sellers. But nobody knew them, and they could think only of each other.

Franco and Nico went off to buy ice creams, while Joanne stretched out on the sand. She needed time to think, time to come to terms with the new person she was this morning.

She felt more physically alive than ever before. The colours of the world had a new vividness, the air was like champagne, and she knew what she'd been born for.

She could see now that if Franco had been frozen in time, so had she, frozen to her love of many years ago. From her new perspective it seemed more of a teenage infatuation with its emphasis on being chosen and loved. But now she loved him as a woman and wanted to give more than to receive. There was nothing she wouldn't do for him, no matter what the cost to herself.

The others returned. She accepted an ice cream and joined in the conversation with half her attention.

Inwardly she was considering her lover, the length of his legs, the straightness of his back, the proud carriage of his head and shoulders. From here she passed to his narrow hips, flat stomach and powerful thighs, but these evoked too many memories from the night before, and she began to blush.

She blushed ever harder when he caught her eye, and she knew he'd guessed her thoughts. But his own thoughts were the same. His reflective smile told her that.

'Please, Papa, can we go into the water now?' Nico pleaded.

Franco rose. 'Are you coming with us?' he asked Joanne.

'No, I'll sunbathe a bit longer,' she said, stretching out comfortably. She wanted some more time to herself, and they too needed to be without her sometimes.

She watched fondly as they ran into the water, the child's hand clasped firmly in the man's. They began to romp together, Franco tossing his son into the air, letting him fall into the water with a splash, but always there with his strong hands to hold him again. Each time Nico would beg eagerly, 'More, Papa.'

The sun was brilliant, gleaming off the water and dazzling Joanne, so that she had to squint to see them. The details disappeared and the two figures became shapes moving against the light. Glittering droplets of water cascaded over them.

Then something occurred to her that made her smile fade, to be replaced by a look of intense concentration. She reached for her bag and pulled out her sketch-pad. She began to make strong, dramatic strokes, seeking to capture the essence of those fast-moving figures.

She became oblivious to her surroundings, oblivious

to everything but the excitement mounting in her. She knew what she was doing was good. It was full of life and conviction, and it was infused by her love for the man and the child. She covered page after page, carried away by a creative urge such as she hadn't known since her student days, when she'd still thought of herself as an artist.

At last she looked up to find Franco and Nico running up the beach. Some deep instinct made her hide the sketch-pad. She wasn't ready to talk about what had happened, even with Franco.

'Shall we go and get some food?' Franco asked when they reached her.

'No, I think I'll take a dip myself now,' Joanne said, getting quickly to her feet. 'There's no need to come with me.'

She wanted to be alone to think, so she swam strongly out into the water, then turned to face the shore. Father and son were tossing a large ball to each other. The light was behind her now, and she could see them clearly. She trod water, her eyes fixed on them, while her brain acted like a camera, the shutter going fast. Click! Franco dived for the ball, his bronzed body graceful against the sand. Click! Nico raced along the beach, hopping and skipping with glee. Click! They were running side by side, the man pulling back to let the boy win the race. Click! Click! Click! Picture after picture imprinted itself on her brain, while she went dizzy with the thrilling thing that was happening.

They had lunch at a little *trattoria*. She ate and drank whatever was put before her, and took only a mechanical part in the conversation. Her mind was filled with bright pictures. Her two menfolk regarded her in consternation. They were used to having her whole attention.

'Is anything wrong?' Franco asked.

'No, everything's wonderfully right,' she told him. 'I've been doing some drawing, and I'm pleased with the way it came out.'

But she wouldn't tell them any more. It was too soon, and she wasn't yet sure.

But Nico's interest had been caught, and before they returned to the beach he dived into a newsagent and begged Franco to buy him a sketch-book. 'Like *Zia's.*'

'I'll get it,' Joanne said, delighted.

They spent the afternoon sketching together. As she'd thought, Nico's drawing showed signs of real skill.

'What's that?' he asked, watching her bring a face to life.

'That's my grandfather, and your great grandfather,' she told him. 'He was a talented artist, and we both get it from him.'

'You look like him,' Nico said, studying the picture.

'Yes, I inherited his looks too. So did your mother.'

'Did you and Mama live together when you were little girls?' Nico asked.

'Not until I was six.' She related the story of her mother's death and how Rosemary had virtually adopted her, and he listened eagerly.

From there she passed onto other memories of their childhood. Nico listened with shining eyes to the tale of the gang that had bullied her at school until Rosemary had come to the rescue, and their kitten who'd gone missing, so that they'd had to hunt for him all night.

'We found him on a patch of waste ground, in a big

pipe,' she remembered. 'We called him, but he was too scared to move, so she had to crawl in and get him. It was a terrible squeeze.'

'But Mama said that was you,' Nico objected. 'She told me about the kitten, and she said she was too big to squeeze through the pipe, so you had to do it.'

'No, it was her,' Joanne protested. 'I'm sure it was—wasn't it?' She covered her eyes, trying to picture the scene. 'I remember her crawling in—maybe she did have to come out again—I don't know, I thought it was her.'

'Does it really matter?' Franco asked gently. 'You were both prepared to do it to save the little cat.'

'No, it doesn't matter at all,' she agreed. 'I do remember that Aunt Elsie was mad at both of us for being out so late. Rosemary insisted that it was her fault, because she was the elder. She was always protecting me.'

'Me too,' Nico said. 'I broke a window once, and she told Papa it was her, because I shouldn't have thrown the ball so near the house.' He took a quick glance at his father. 'Sorry, Papa.'

'I guessed,' he said with a grin. 'I used to get mad at her. I'd say, "How can I teach him to do right if you always shield him?" And she'd say, "If he knows he's loved, he'll know how to do right."'

He held out his arm and Nico scrambled into the curve, to be held tight against his father's body. Joanne watched them contentedly. Something had happened this afternoon, something for which there were no words, but which made everything better.

They drove home slowly, arriving in the dusk. This time Franco declined the Terrinis' hospitality, choosing

to cook part of the supper himself, and giving Joanne
a chance to show off what she'd learned.

She lay awake for a long time that night, waiting for
Franco to come to her, but he didn't, and her heart
sank. Of course, with Nico there, they had to be cir-
cumspect, but she couldn't help feeling that he would
have managed somehow, if he'd really wanted to. She
fell asleep feeling despondent.

She awoke very early. Dawn was creeping across the
lake, creating silhouettes, dark at first then tipped with
silver. She watched, motionless, thrilled by the play of
light and shade, until she couldn't bear to sit still any
longer. Pulling on some clothes, she took her sketch-
pad and slipped away.

On the beach she plunged into an orgy of sketching,
while her mind's eye saw the pictures that would result.
The fishermen were emerging from their houses, preparing to start up the boats. A few strokes caught the
sweep of their powerful movements. She could fill in
the details later, now that she'd caught the essence.
When she was satisfied she crept back into the house,
returned to bed and fell instantly into a contented sleep.

She awoke to the feel of Franco's lips on hers, and
his arms around her.

'Good morning,' he whispered against her mouth.

The room was full of warm light, as though the day
was far advanced.

'Franco—'

'Hush, not now.' He pulled back the sheet, which
was all that covered her, and drew her naked body next
to his.

'But Nico—' she said urgently.

'Nico has gone fishing. He'll be away all day. I had
to have a day alone with you. Did I do right?'

'Mmm, yes. You did exactly right.'

It was hard to speak for he was caressing her already, exciting her with subtle movements. She understood the message of those movements now, knew the pleasure that was to come, and responded with eager anticipation. He understood and laughed at her gently.

'Not so fast,' he teased. 'We have all the time in the world.'

'We can't be sure,' she said urgently. 'Maybe there's only now.'

'You're right. We must treat every moment as the last. Come to me, my love.'

My love. Her heart treasured the words. She was his love, as he was hers. She gave herself up to him with joy, offering all the love in her heart, for now and for ever. And it was given back to her a thousandfold. Now the union of their flesh felt like the union of their hearts.

When passion was slaked and they lay contentedly in each other's arms he asked, just a shade too casually, 'Did you miss me last night?'

'Not a bit,' she said with dignity.

'Little liar! At least, I hope you are. I wanted to come to you, but Nico was restless and I had to be with him. This morning I almost begged the Terrinis to take him out, so that we could have the day alone together.'

'I'm so glad you did,' she murmured, snuggling against him, and immediately dozing off.

She awoke first, and slipped gently out from under his arm. Franco was sprawled across the bed, his big, relaxed body speaking eloquently of the satiety of love. She knew a passionate urge to capture that on paper, and began sketching madly.

Again she felt the thrill of being mistress of her own creation. It was different from the excitement that had so recently possessed her, but just as satisfying in a different way. She became so absorbed that she didn't notice Franco had woken and was looking at her with interest.

'Can I see?' he asked.

'You moved!' she cried in anguish.

'I'm sorry.' He lay down again.

'No, further to your left,' she said, frowning. 'Bit more—bit more. That's it!'

After a while he said, 'Am I allowed to speak?'

'As long as you don't move.'

'I saw you slip out onto the beach this morning. I kept thinking you'd look up and notice me, but you never did.'

'Uh-uh!' She was making rapid movement.

'Did you hear what I said?' he asked. There was a slight edge on his voice and she looked at him quickly.

'I'm sorry,' he said at once. 'I didn't mean to snap. It's just that—' he wore a self-mocking grin '—I'm not used to being with a woman who ignores me.'

'But I'm not ignoring you,' she protested. 'I've been drawing you for ages. I mean—'

'Quite. You've been drawing me, but as a man I haven't existed. Light and shade, yes. But as a man, no.'

'Oh, dear,' she said, mortified. 'I hadn't realized. I got so excited with this—'

'Never mind. It's probably good for my vanity,' he said with a touch of ruefulness. 'Now may I see?'

She put the sketch-pad into his outstretched hand and he studied the pictures.

'Who are you being this time?' he asked after a while. 'Leonardo, Michelangelo—?'

'This time I'm being me,' Joanne said.

He made an alert movement, and she knew that he'd immediately understood the true meaning of her words. He began to go through the pictures again, seeing them with new eyes, nodding as what had happened became plain to him. When he looked up at her his eyes mirrored her own sense of triumph.

'E miracolo,' he said.

He'd said it exactly. A miracle. Something that happened without apparent reason, at a moment of its own choosing. Beyond logical understanding. The dream she'd longed for all these years had finally come true. And the best thing of all was sharing it with him, knowing that he felt its full significance to her, because of the understanding that was growing between them.

'But why now, at this moment?' he asked.

She could have told him that it was because their love had completed her as a woman, and therefore as an artist. That it was this completeness that enabled her to sing in her own authentic voice, instead of echoing the voices of others. But she kept silent for the moment. There were secrets that must wait for another time, and secrets that could not be told at all. She wasn't yet sure which one this was.

He cooked the lunch himself, serving her with a flourish. Afterwards they went back to bed and lay in each other's arms, not making love but talking in slow, contented voices. 'You have recalled me to life,' he said. 'I was in a dead place, and glad to be so, because the one I loved was there. But now, another one I love has shown the path back, and the world is beautiful again.'

'Another that you love?' she whispered longingly.

'Will you believe me when I say that I love you? *You,* not a shadow. There are no explanations, just the feeling. And what I feel is that I love you more than my own life.'

'I want so much to believe you.'

'When you went away—when I drove you away—I cursed myself for my own stupidity. You'd filled the house with grace, and brought a peace to my heart I'd thought never to know again.'

'But that was because I reminded you of her.'

'I thought so at first. But as time went by I found my memories were all of you, things you'd said and done that weren't like her at all. I couldn't stop thinking of you, wondering if you hated me, whether I'd thrown away any hope for us.

'It all came back from years ago. You were just a kid. But you were delightful, and I was very fond of you.'

'You never noticed me.'

'I never tried to seduce you,' he corrected. 'That's different. You were too special to be one of my light-o'-loves. And you don't need to tell me that I had too many—'

'*Far* too many.' They laughed together.

'Yes, but I was already growing up, seeking a woman I could truly love. If I hadn't met Rosemary, I think it would have been you, one day. But not then. You were too young, and we weren't ready for each other as we are now.

'But I did meet her and loved her, and thought of nobody else while she lived. Not even you.'

'I'm glad. I wouldn't have wanted to take anything away from Rosemary.'

'You didn't. But now—' A shadow crossed his face.
'What is it, Franco?'

The shadow flickered and was gone. 'They say that a man who loves more than once somehow chooses the same woman every time. I love you for the things you share with Rosemary—not your face, which grows less like hers the more I know you; but your sweetness and compassion, the way your arms open to welcome life, the way you love without thinking of yourself.

'But I love also the things that are different in you, even your "other world", the place you go to when you take up a pencil and forget I exist.'

'And you don't mind? I don't believe that.'

'I mind,' he admitted with a grin. 'I don't say I like it, but I can love it, because it's you. But that's recent. While you were away, and I was coming to my senses, I began to realize what a fatal mistake I'd made. And yet I couldn't come to you because my thoughts were still confused and I didn't know what to say.

'It was true that Nico wanted you for his birthday, but—' his grin mocked himself '—if it hadn't been that, I'd have found something else. I had to get you back, and start again. I was a little too sure of myself as I drove to Turin. And I found you in Leo's arms.'

'I've told you about that—'

'I know, but at the time it gave me a nasty shock. And he kept turning up.'

'He won't turn up again. I don't think he really cares about me anyway.'

'To hell with what he cares about! Tell me again that *he* means nothing to *you*.'

She slipped her arms contentedly about his neck. 'How would you like me to tell you?'

'In whichever way you think will be most convincing.'

'You could always listen while I telephone him,' she teased.

'I was thinking of something much more convincing than that. Come here and let me show you...'

She responded passionately, rejoicing to be in his arms, forgetting all else. Now that her dream had come true she wanted to savour it every moment, and rediscover her joy with every sweet caress. He loved her gently, patiently at first, then with vigour and purpose, and finally with a tenderness that almost made her want to weep. The world held nothing better than this.

It was only much later that she listened to the haunting, uneasy echo in her head. It came from the shadow that had crossed his face, and it warned her that in the midst of their happiness there was something ominously wrong.

A few days later they packed everything into the car and headed for home. By the time they were on the last stretch the sun was setting, casting a coral glow over the land. Nico and his two canine friends were sound asleep in the back. Joanne turned slightly in her seat, drinking in the sight of her lover. She was filled with wonder at the marvellous thing that had happened to her.

He loved her. It was unbelievable, but he loved her. Not a pale echo of another love, but her, Joanne. He had said so, and he was a man of his word.

Without taking his eyes off the road, Franco reached over and took her hand, to draw it to his lips.

'Will you marry me soon?' he asked.

'As soon as you like, my darling. I must finish my work for the Antoninis, but that won't take long.'

'I long to have you as my wife.'

'I'm almost frightened,' she said. 'Nobody is allowed to be this happy. Something will spoil it.'

'I don't believe it,' he said firmly. 'We will make a world together that nothing can destroy.'

She remembered that he knew all about seeing his joy snatched away in a moment, and decided to say no more. But her uneasiness persisted.

The last mile. The light was fast fading, but she could recognize the way home. *Her* home now, a place that was warm and welcoming to her. Franco was right. It was foolish to give way to groundless fears.

The car slowed to a crawl and glided between the gate posts. There up ahead was the house, ablaze with golden light. As they drew up they could clearly hear the sound of two female voices, raised in dispute. One of them belonged to Celia. The other, Joanne recognized instantly.

She tried to ignore the cold hand that seized the pit of her stomach. Her fears had come rushing back and she knew that something terrible was about to happen.

She understood why when they entered the house, and Franco's mother rose to greet them.

CHAPTER ELEVEN

'GOOD evening, my son,' Sophia said, smiling coldly.

She was older, thinner, harder. Her face was a little more lined and a lot more sour. When Franco went to her, her arms closed around him possessively.

He greeted his mother affectionately, and Sophia seemed to return the affection, but her eyes on Joanne were cold as stones. She enveloped her in a formal embrace.

'It's delightful to see you again, after so long,' she said. 'And dear little Nico. Put that dirty dog down and give your grandmama a big hug.'

She pulled the reluctant child against her. Nico returned her hug obediently, but without enthusiasm, and afterwards he slipped away quickly, scooping up the pups as he went.

'I'll do Nico's unpacking,' Joanne told Franco.

'There's no need.' Sophia restrained her with a chilly hand on her arm. 'It isn't the job of a *guest* to unpack for my grandchild.'

'Joanne is being kind,' Franco said. 'She knows that you and I wish to be alone together. How are you, Mama?'

He opened his arms to her again, but Sophia evaded his embrace. 'One moment.' She waylaid Nico before he could mount the stairs, and removed the pups from him. 'We don't allow dogs upstairs. In fact dogs belong outside.'

160

She took Pepe and Zaza to the door and shoved them out.

'Papa lets me keep them indoors,' Nico said indignantly.

'Not now, Nico,' Franco said. 'Go upstairs.'

Nico stuck out his lower lip rebelliously, but Joanne calmed him with a touch on his shoulder. His answering smile wasn't lost on Sophia whose eyes became, if possible, harder than ever.

'I don't like her,' Nico muttered as they unpacked.

'Shh, Nico, you shouldn't say things like that.'

'But she didn't like Mama. She doesn't like anybody.'

Joanne soon learned that Sophia had arrived two hours earlier and contrived to upset the entire estate. The meal Celia had lovingly cooked for their return had been pronounced unsuitable and a new menu drawn up.

'She stands over me in the kitchen as though I'd never cooked before in my life,' Celia seethed. 'Everything has to be done her way. But her way is not my way, and it's my kitchen.'

'Why did she come here now?' Joanne asked.

'She telephone yesterday, and when she find that Signor Franco is at the lake with you, she say, "I see", in a special way that mean she is angry.'

'I remember the way she used to say that,' Joanne said with foreboding. 'It used to send shivers down everyone's spine.'

'Sì. Shivers,' Celia agreed, but then became more cheerful. 'But, after all, if you and Signor Franco— well, what can she do?'

'I wish I knew,' Joanne murmured. Her uneasiness was increasing by the moment.

Supper was a tense meal. Celia had done her best to change everything to Sophia's orders, but it had been a last-minute rush. Sophia praised every dish in a tinkling, silver voice, but always with a suggestion for improvement that turned praise to blame.

Franco tried hard to give his mother's thoughts a more cheerful direction, asking about her husband and her two stepchildren.

'They are all well, my son. None of them gives me a moment's anxiety. It seemed the right moment to pay a visit to my true family.'

'That's good of you, Mama, but you've no need to be anxious about Nico or me.'

'That, perhaps, is a matter of opinion. But we can discuss the matter later. *Signorina,* did you enjoy yourself at Lake Garda?'

'Mama,' Franco protested, 'you can't suddenly start calling Joanne "*signorina*". You've known her for years, and she's part of the family.'

'Oh, yes, of course. Forgive me, *signorina,* but it's been so long since we met that I'd forgotten that you are, in some slight way, connected with us. In fact, you've been away for so long that I wonder why you returned now.'

'My career has often taken me to the other side of the world,' Joanne said, determinedly polite.

'Ah, yes, your career. I remember how determined you were to be a great artist. These days a woman must decide which is more important to her: her career, or a family.'

'She doesn't always have to make a choice,' Joanne said, speaking politely and refusing to let herself be needled.

'Really? I would have thought that there was always

some sort of choice to be made. Nobody gets everything in this world, do they?'

'No, *signora,* they don't,' Joanne said with a small flash of temper. The words might have meant nothing, but the goaded look she gave Sophia contained a challenge, and the flash in the older woman's eyes showed that she understood.

It had been a long day, and Nico's eyes were beginning to close. As soon as supper was over Joanne said, 'Come on, darling. Off to bed.'

'I won't put a guest to so much trouble,' Sophia said, rising instantly.

'Let Joanne do it, Mama,' Franco said. 'She's been looking after Nico while we were away.'

'But now his Grandmama is here,' Sophia said with a smile that was like the drawing of battle lines. Her claw-like hand fixed itself on Nico's shoulder.

'Let Joanne take him,' Franco said firmly. 'We so rarely see each other, Mama, that I don't want to lose a moment with you.' He took her hand in his, a gesture of affection that nonetheless prevented her from interfering with the others.

When she'd put Nico to bed Joanne returned downstairs long enough to say, 'I think I'll retire now. You'll wish to be alone. Goodnight.'

She left before Franco had the chance to kiss her, knowing it would only make Sophia worse if he did, and triumphant if he didn't. But she gave him a smile to show that she understood his predicament, and knew that Sophia had seen that, too.

Through a restless night she tried to believe she was worrying about nothing. Sophia could throw all the tantrums she pleased. Franco had dealt with them before, and knew how to ride out the storm.

But this time there was something different, and she was beginning to be afraid that she knew what it was.

In the early morning she slipped out and made her way on foot through the garden and down the path under the trees. She plucked some wild flowers along the way, until she had a pretty bunch in her hand.

Rosemary's grave looked peaceful in the early morning light. Joanne dropped on one knee to brush some of the long grass away, and laid the flowers down. She spoke to Rosemary, not aloud, but silently, in her heart.

I love him, darling. He loves me, and I know I can make him happy. It's only that—you don't mind, do you?

She heard a step behind her and turned to see Sophia watching her coolly.

'I followed you here,' the older woman said, 'to find out how much of a fool you really are. I wanted to see you offer flowers to the woman who took him from you—oh, yes, I knew you loved him.'

'She didn't take him from me,' Joanne said. 'He was always hers, from the moment they met.'

'And he is hers still,' Sophia said bitterly. 'He'll be hers for ever. There was never anything so strong as her grip on his heart. She even turned him against his mother.'

'Rosemary wouldn't have done that.'

'No? I tell you he drove me out of his house to please her. His own mother!'

Sophia came nearer. Her eyes were glittering. 'Don't ever delude yourself that he loves you. To him you're an imitation, nothing more. His heart is still in there.' She flung out an arm to the grave. 'She bewitched him, and he will never be free.'

'I don't believe you,' Joanne said breathlessly. 'I

knew Rosemary. She was a wonderful, generous woman who gave all of herself.'

'She was a woman who took everything, because she could never be satisfied. And she wants everything still. You can't fight her. *She will never give him up.*'

Tight-lipped, Joanne turned to leave.

'That's right, run away from the truth,' Sophia jeered.

'I'm not running away, but I won't stay and argue with you, Sophia. Franco loves me, and I love him. And I'm not going to become the victim of your hate.'

She walked away without a backward glance. Her head was held up at a proud angle, and she didn't look back. But she was trembling.

'I don't believe it,' she said to Franco later that day. 'Your mother says Rosemary made you throw her out, but that can't be true.'

'Of course it isn't true,' Franco said wryly. 'Mama was the only person I knew who didn't like Rosemary. I think she was jealous because I loved her so much. And then—two women in the same kitchen—it was the old story.

'Rosemary did her best, but Mama made a fight of it, always trying to bully her, saying things to needle her. Once she made a great fuss over something that wasn't really important. I tried to calm her down but she demanded that I take her side. I couldn't do that. Rosemary was my wife, and besides, she was in the right.

'When I wouldn't speak the words Mama wanted to put into my mouth, she declared that since there was no place for her in her son's home—which wasn't true—she would "seek refuge" with her sister in Naples.'

'I can just hear her playing it for all the drama it was worth,' Joanne said wryly.

'I replied that a visit to Naples might be a good idea. I thought she'd stay away a few weeks to clear the air, then return and we could start again.

'But she never returned. In Naples she met Tonio and married him. Now she runs him, his house, his children and his servants, for he's a wealthy man. Tonio dotes on her and gives her everything she wants. But whenever she wants a stick to beat me with I become the heartless son who threw her out of her home.'

'I thought it might be something like that.'

'But—I wish I knew how women's minds work. Why does she tell you how much I loved Rosemary, when she tried to make Rosemary believe that I didn't?'

'Because she's using her to push us apart. She'll say anything she thinks might work, whether she believes it or not.'

Franco slipped an arm about her waist. 'Don't worry, she won't stay long. But while she's here it's best to let her do as she pleases. Then you and I will be free to start our life together.'

'Have you said anything to Nico yet?'

'No, I want to wait until this is over. Mind you, I think he's guessed, and he's thrilled.'

'I'll try to make him happy, Franco.'

'Hey, what about making me happy?' he asked with a smile. 'I'm not doing this for Nico. I'm doing it for me.'

'Sure?'

'If you doubt me I'll have to spend my life making the matter plain to you. Come here, my love.'

He drew her into his arms, and in the tenderness of his kisses she managed to put her fears aside.

The storm didn't break until next day. Joanne went riding with Nico and stayed out with him as long as possible, unwilling to face the atmosphere that Sophia seemed to carry with her. When they returned he raced off to play with his friends. As she went indoors she could hear the old woman's angry voice carrying.

'What you're proposing to do is a scandal. Everyone is shocked.'

'I don't think so.' Franco was speaking in the easy-going way that he habitually used to cool her down. 'Everyone on the estate is pleased at what's happening.'

'They're pleased that you're making a fool of yourself over a girl who happens to look like your wife?'

'It's not her face,' Franco said at once. 'Joanne is only herself, and it's Joanne that I love. Don't try to convince her otherwise. She knows me too well.'

'And why does she look so like Rosemary?' Sophia snapped. 'Because she's her cousin. Have you thought what you're doing, marrying another from that family? Suppose she too has a weak heart? These things can be hereditary.'

'That's true,' Joanne said, stepping into the room. 'Rosemary inherited her weakness from her mother. But she and I were related through our fathers, who were brothers. I'm not connected to her mother at all. And I'm perfectly strong.'

'Strong enough to step into a dead woman's shoes, where you have no right,' Sophia sneered.

'That's for Franco to say.'

'You're very confident. You might not be so sure of
yourself if you could have seen him when she died. He
was dead himself, inside. He told me everything was
ended for him. He swore he would never love again,
that he had no *right* to love again. He still has no right.
And he knows why.' She turned on Franco. 'How can
you forget your wife so soon, *when it was you who
killed her?*'

Franco's face had a ghastly pallor. 'I didn't kill her,'
he cried out.

'As good as. It was you who wanted more children,
you she was trying to please.'

'As God is my witness,' he said harshly, 'if I'd
known she was weak I'd never have asked for another
child. She was everything to me. Would I have risked
her life if I'd known?'

'And why didn't you know? Why did she hide the
truth? Because she knew you didn't want to hear it.'

She waited for his answer, but he only looked at her
with eyes that had seen hell. Joanne bit back a cry. She
longed to help him, but even her love couldn't conquer
his demons for him. Only he could do that.

'She gave her life to please you,' Sophia said with
a kind of triumph. 'How can you make her sacrifice
count for nothing? If you were dead, would she love
again, in a year? Ten years? Ever? You know that she
wouldn't.'

'For God's sake!' Franco whispered. 'What are you
trying to do?'

'Trying to make you see the truth of what you're
doing, before it's too late.'

'No,' Franco said in a firmer voice. 'You want to
make trouble between us, just as you tried to make
trouble during my marriage. Understand me, Mama, I

won't allow it. I don't know why you feel you must tear things down, but I won't let you do it.'

Sophia regarded him with pity. 'Do you think you can silence the truth like that?'

Franco's voice was steady. 'I want you to leave, Mama.'

Sophia met his eyes, and gave a very thin smile.

'Very well, my son. I will leave at once.'

Joanne was surprised by this easy capitulation, but only for a moment. She'd seen the hint of triumph in the older woman's manner, and it told her the worst.

Sophia was leaving because she had no further need to stay.

When Franco returned from seeing his mother off at the airport he went in search of Joanne, and found her in her room. What he saw there made him stop on the threshold.

'What the devil are you doing?' he demanded, staring at the open suitcases that were filling up.

'I'm getting ready to leave.'

'Yes, of course,' he said after a moment. 'You must return to the Antoninis and finish your work for them before we can be married.'

'No, I'm leaving for good.' She looked up at him with a ravaged face. 'We can't be married, Franco. Not now, or for a long time. Maybe not ever.'

'That's nonsense!' he said violently. 'Of course we're going to be married. I thought you had more sense than to believe what my mother said.'

'It's you that believes it. She's done what she meant to. You feel guilty, just as she wants.'

It was just a fraction too long before he spoke, and then his voice was forced.

'That's absurd. You heard me tell her that she was wasting her time trying to make trouble between us.'

'Yes, I heard you tell her. And you're right. She can't really make trouble between us, because I'll always love you, and I think you'll always love me. But we can't marry, because whatever you say, whatever you try to believe, your mind is troubled because of Rosemary.

'I've seen it, in odd moments when you thought I wasn't noticing. We've been happy, and you've suddenly remembered that *her* happiness is over for ever. Then you've told yourself it was your fault, and you've wondered what right you have to be happy.'

The look he gave her was one of desperation. 'Why do you talk like this?' he demanded. 'Why don't you help me fight it?'

'Because I'm not sure it can be fought. You're not to blame for Rosemary's death, but the rest is true. You did share a remarkable love. You felt like two halves of one person, which means that if she's dead you should be dead too. But you're not dead. You've returned to life and you're ready to move on, except that part of you doesn't believe you have any right to. Sophia exploited that. But the real problem is in there.' She tapped him gently on the breast.

He turned away and leaned his arm against the window, resting his forehead on it. Joanne was torn apart, longing to help him. It would be so easy to give in and marry him quickly. But they would never have a peaceful moment.

'It's just a mood,' he said at last. 'It was bound to cross my mind, but it'll pass. Do you doubt that I love you?'

'No, I know you love me. In a way, that may be just the problem—'

'Yes,' he said, picking up her thought instantly in the way she found so lovable. 'If I loved you less, I'd have less cause for guilt. It's because my love for you is so total, so overwhelming, that it feels like a betrayal.' A shudder possessed him. 'It's true that I killed her,' he said in agony.

'No, it isn't true.'

'She died trying to please me. I didn't know that her health was so bad, but I should have known. Many times I asked her, ''When will we have another child, beloved?'''

'And she kept her secret. That was her decision.'

'Because she thought only of me, of my wishes. Perhaps if I hadn't pressed her she could have told me it was impossible. Why did she feel she couldn't tell me? How did I fail her? I loved her so much, and yet I failed her. And because of that failure she's dead.'

'You're right. I've asked myself many times how I can put her sacrifice behind me, and find a new life. I've lain with you beside me, listening to your breathing, and I've kissed you in your sleep, longing to be shown the way, because to part from you would break my heart.' He seemed to shake himself out of an unhappy dream. 'But that will pass,' he added quickly.

'I don't think so. I think you loved her too much for it to pass. But, my darling, there's something else. It isn't just you that feels guilty, but me too. I'll tell you something that I've kept a secret until now. I fell in love with you years ago, but you loved Rosemary, and married her. When she died I still loved you, but I couldn't come here then. Don't you see why?'

'I think so...' he said slowly.

'I would have felt wrong to come rushing out here trying to take what was hers. That's how I thought of you—hers. In a way, I still do. All these years I've envied Rosemary because she had you, and then when I could have—well, I just couldn't. And even now—' she sighed '—it feels like stealing. I know it's crazy—'

'Then we're both crazy,' he said heavily.

'Maybe when someone's been given such a precious gift, it's something that can only come once, and they mustn't ask for more—' Joanne broke off because her voice had become thick with tears. What she was doing was tearing her apart, but something stronger than herself told her it must be done.

'And what about Nico?' he demanded suddenly. 'How will we explain to him that he's losing you? I told you I wasn't marrying you for his sake, and it was true. But now I'll say to you, marry me for Nico's sake. Forget all we've said here today and think only of him.'

'It's no use, my darling,' she said helplessly. 'The problem would still be there, and we'd end up tearing ourselves and each other apart. Nico would see that, and he'd suffer more than if I went now.'

She couldn't bear the hurt in his face. She opened her arms to enfold him, and he came to her blindly. They stood for a long moment holding each other, silent, motionless.

'I can't let you go,' he said at last. 'Don't ask me to do that.'

'It might not be for ever. One day—'

'You don't get a miracle back once you've thrown it away. If we part now, it will be for ever. I feel it.'

'But there's no way out. What we're really asking is for Rosemary to give us her blessing. And even she can't manage that.' Suddenly she was shaken by the misery of what she had to do. 'Hold me, my love. Hold me and love me…just once more.'

They loved gently, with tenderness greater than passion, storing memories for the long years apart. When they became one she told herself that she would always be one with him, always belong to him, body and heart and soul, although she might never see him again.

'My love,' he whispered. 'Always…always…'

And her heart answered, *Always.*

She was glad now that they hadn't told Nico of their marriage plans, so there was no need to tell him that the plans were shattered. He took her departure calmly, evidently assuming that she would be back soon, as had happened before. Some time Franco would have to tell him that she would never return, but by that time perhaps his bond to her would have loosened a little.

When they said goodbye Nico gave her a picture he had drawn, showing a man, a woman and a little boy.

'It's us,' he explained. 'So you don't forget us.'

'I'll never forget you, darling,' she told him, trying not to break down.

Franco drove her to the station and waited while she boarded the train. She felt as if she were dying, and his eyes told her that it was the same with him.

When the train was ready to depart it swept over her with awful finality, what she was doing, that it was for ever.

'Franco—' She reached out to him wildly.

'For God's sake, go!' he said in a shaking voice. 'Leave me alone with my dead.'

CHAPTER TWELVE

'JUST another week,' Maria pleaded. 'Please, we want you to stay.'

'But I've finished all your pictures,' Joanne said. 'And you've paid me. I've no excuse for staying.'

'Except that we want you. I give a party next week and show the pictures off, and you must be there to explain them,' Maria said, triumphant at having finally thought of an excuse.

'All right, I'll stay until then.'

'*Bene*. And by then, who knows? He may have called.'

'He isn't going to call, Maria. It's over. And it was as much my decision as his. More perhaps.'

'If you gave up such a man as that, you are *stupida*.' Maria declared, leaving the room indignantly.

'Yes,' Joanne murmured. 'I am *stupida*. But I can't help it. It would never have worked. Not without Rosemary's blessing. And she can't give us that now.'

She'd returned to Turin three weeks ago, and many times since then she'd pictured herself going back to Franco, marrying him, forgetting all for love. And they would be happy for a while. But then the shadow hanging over them would grow bigger until it destroyed them. Rosemary had given her husband everything, and then sacrificed her life. And he couldn't accept such a sacrifice with a shrug. He was a man of honour, with an overgrown conscience. The more he loved Joanne, the more guilty he would feel.

Maybe one day he would feel that his debts were paid and he was entitled to be happy. But that day would be a long time coming.

Now that the Antoninis' pictures were all done she had only her own painting to pass the time. Once this had been a dispiriting process, underlining her limitations. But the inspiration she'd discovered at the lake had stayed with her. It was as if her love for Franco had completed her, not only as a woman, but as an artist.

It made no difference that they'd lost each other. The love they'd shared had been deep and passionate, giving each of them an extra dimension, and nothing would ever be the same for either of them. If she never saw him again, never heard his voice or saw his eyes soften as they rested on her, still he'd left his legacy in her life. And because of it, she would endure and be stronger.

But then she wondered about what she had left him. Was there any way their love could be a strength to him through the years apart, or had she merely abandoned him to more bitterness? When she thought of that it took all her strength not to call him.

She completed the pictures of him and Nico. Then, half fearing, she began work on the fishing village, and found that the charm was still powerful even when Franco wasn't the subject. The pictures took shape under her skilful fingers: confident, imaginative, but above all her own.

She was a true artist at last. And Franco's love had done this for her.

An art expert came to the villa to inspect her reproductions. He turned out to be her old tutor from the academy in Turin. He pronounced the copies excellent, and then, at Maria's insistence, examined Joanne's own paintings. After a long silence he looked up at her with a curious smile.

'So! You found the missing ''something'' at last?'

'Yes, I found it,' she agreed.

'And now it will never leave you.'

He told her to contact him when she had more work to show, promising to speak to a friend in Rome who owned a gallery. Joanne tucked his card away in a safe place. A new part of her life was just beginning. But most valuable of all were the words, 'now it will never leave you.' As long as she lived, she would have something of Franco's, although he himself might never know.

As she'd promised, she stayed for Maria's party, and every time the telephone rang she flinched. Then told herself to be sensible, when it wasn't him.

Leo rang her, and she finally managed to convince him that he was wasting his time. Two days later she watched the Asti *palio* on television, and saw him speed to his long-delayed victory.

At the party she did her hosts proud. She was approached for another commission in the area, but she declined. She could never come back here again.

She finished her packing late next afternoon and took a last look around her room. Vito and Maria were driving her to the airport to catch the evening plane to England, and she must go down to them at any moment.

Somewhere in the house she heard the shrill of the phone, but by now she'd trained herself not to react. Vito looked in to help her with her baggage, and they went down the stairs and out to the car.

'Where is Maria?' he demanded with husbandly exasperation. 'Isn't she coming with us?'

'I think she's on the phone—no, there she is.'

Maria came flying out of the front door, her face wreathed in smiles. 'It's him,' she shrieked triumphantly to Joanne.

'Maria—who?'

'Signor Farelli. He must talk to you, very urgent. Hurry.'

Joanne ran back into the house and snatched up the phone. When she'd said 'Hallo,' she held her breath. She would surely know from Franco's tone whether this was good news or bad.

But he sounded strange and unlike himself. 'I'm sorry to trouble you,' he said stiffly, 'but I must ask you to return here.'

'Franco, what is it?'

'I can't tell you over the phone. Can you come at once?'

'Of course I will.'

'Thank you.' He hung up.

'Well?' Maria demanded in agony.

'He wants to see me, but he won't say why.'

The old couple were as overjoyed as if she were their own daughter. They almost pushed her into the car, Vito handed her the keys and told her to be off.

'Invite us to the wedding,' Maria called.

But, try as she would, Joanne could extract no message of reassurance from Franco's voice. If anything he'd sounded curt. And yet he wanted her to come back, and the ache of misery in her heart seemed to lift a little.

She resisted the temptation to drive fast, but she was eager to see him again at the first possible moment. As she rounded the last bend into the valley she saw a figure standing on the peak, watching the road by which she must come. It was too far away for the man's face to be clear, but her heart told her it was Franco. As soon as he saw her car he mounted his horse and galloped off in the direction of the house. Whatever was the matter, he was so anxious for her arrival that he had been watching for her.

He was waiting by the front door as she drew up, his face dark and full of tension. He didn't open his arms, attempt to kiss her, or give her any kind of welcome. They might have been distant acquaintances, except that he looked pale and ill, as though the weeks apart had tortured him too.

'Forgive me for demanding you at a moment's notice,' he said, 'but something has happened, and I need you.'

'Nico—'

'Nico is well. He's staying with friends today. I have to talk to you alone.'

'Franco, don't keep me in suspense. What is this all about?'

'Come with me.'

He led her into the house and upstairs to his room. A large box stood in the middle of the floor. It was open, and the contents were scattered all around, as though someone had been going through them hastily.

'They were her things,' Franco said. 'When she died I locked them away. I couldn't bear even to go through them. But today Nico asked me about them, and I opened the box. I found this.' He held out a cream, sealed envelope. Taking it, Joanne could feel that it contained several sheets of paper. Her own name was written on the outside in Rosemary's hand.

'She wrote that just before she died,' Franco said.

'You've read it?'

'Of course not. It's sealed. But that paper is used by the hospital. It has the hospital name stamped on the envelope. She wrote it while she was there.'

His eyes burned her.

'Don't you see what it means? She knew she was dying. She must have meant that letter to be given to you after her death. For God's sake, read it. And if you can, tell me what it says.'

With shaking hands Joanne opened the envelope, and read aloud Rosemary's last words to her.

'My darling Joanne,

If you ever read this, it will be because I'm not here to talk to you any more, and there are things I so much want you to know.

I took a gamble with this pregnancy, but every day I've been afraid it wouldn't come off. Yesterday my heart began to give out, and they brought me here, to this hospital. I know they expect me to have another attack.

I dreamed of growing old with Franco and seeing our children become strong and wise. Now I think it will never happen, and I must take care of him in the only way I can.

I want you to come out to Italy, and look after Franco, and Nico. You see, darling, I know your secret. I know you love him, and that's why you've stayed away from us. I've known ever since I visited you in England. You never told me in words, but the truth shone from you whenever I spoke his name. You love him, and you are the only person I can entrust him to.

Nico, too, will be all right with you. I used to watch him snuggle happily in your arms, and I know you'll keep him safe.

I hope Franco comes to love you, and that you will marry. He'll resist, because he's a man of honour, and he'll feel he's betraying me. But that's not so. He gave me all his love while I needed it, and when I need it no longer I want him to be free to love again. Perhaps you can teach him to understand. I hope so.

I thought of writing all this to him, but it wouldn't do. He needs to come to the idea gradually, when he's ready. I leave that to you. You'll know how to pick the moment.

Goodbye, my dearest. I entrust my two most precious treasures to your safe keeping. Be happy, and teach my poor Franco that it isn't wrong for him to find a new life with you. I know I'll always have my own corner of his heart, and you're too generous to grudge it me. The rest I gladly give to you.'

Joanne's voice faltered, and for a moment her eyes were blurred with tears as she thought of great-hearted Rosemary, whose generosity had never faltered, right to the end.

When she could see again she looked at Franco. He was sitting with his face buried in his hands. She wanted to go to him, but she must wait. There was one last thing.

Rosemary had written:

'You'll find my thoughts to Franco enclosed with this letter. When you think he's ready to hear them, I want you to read them to him yourself.'

'What are her words to me?' Franco said huskily.

It was growing darker. Joanne rose and sat by the window to catch the light. From here she guessed she must present a silhouette to Franco, and probably she seemed more like Rosemary than ever before. She hadn't planned it, but perhaps it was for the best. For one more time she must 'be' Rosemary for him, giving him the last message from the wife he had loved, and whose love for him reached out from beyond the grave.

'It's a short verse,' she said, glancing at the paper. 'It seems that she managed that poem at last. It's called—it's called ''Goodbye''.'

A tremor went through him. 'Read it to me.'

Softly Joanne began to read. As she did so, she felt as though Rosemary were there in the room with them, a strong, tender presence, making her last and greatest gift to those she loved.

'Remember me a little while,
Pause in the orchard where we often walked,
When days were longer and the world was ours.
Say, *"Cara, please!"* one last time, and smile.

From beneath the apple tree,
Glance up to where I once looked down at you.
Wear, just once more,
The look that said I was your love,
And you were mine until my end.
I knew it all the while.

Miss me, but not for long.
I was your joy,
Don't let me be your woe,

So remember me, and smile.
Then let me go.'

When she had finished there was silence. Joanne sat with her head bent, tears falling silently down her cheeks. It was all there, everything that had made Rosemary the person she was: the understanding and compassion, above all the love, stronger than self, stronger than death.

At last Franco rose and came to her. He dropped on his knees beside her and put his arms about her, resting his head against her. He was weeping, and she joined her tears to his, stroking his head. Just now they had no thoughts for themselves. This was Rosemary's moment, and they would give it to her in full measure.

'She loved you so much,' Joanne whispered.

'She loved us both,' he said huskily. 'All this time— I could have sent you that letter when she died.'

'It wouldn't have been the right moment, my darling. We were neither of us ready then.'

He lifted his head to look at her. 'I feel as though a huge weight has gone from my heart.'

'That's how she meant it,' Joanne said. 'That was her gift. We wanted her blessing, and now she's given it to us.'

'To be granted two miracles in one life,' he said softly. 'No man has the right.'

'You have the right to all the best the world has to offer,' she told him. 'And I'm going to give it to you.'

'The best is you. If I have you, I have everything.'

'And you'll have me always. I'll never leave you again.'

He rose to his feet and drew her up and into his arms. 'Promise me that your life is mine, as mine is yours.'

'I promise,' she said. 'Yours. Always. And Rosemary was right. I don't grudge her a place in your heart. That's where she belongs, just as I do. Keep us both safely there, my darling. Now and for ever.'

EPILOGUE

THE trees hang over the marble headstone, their branches heavy with blossom. A winter has come and gone, and the earth is full of new life and hope.

There are fresh flowers there today. Two bouquets of roses lie side by side, one red, one white. A card nestles between them. It bears no name, and contains only two, heartfelt words.

Thank you.

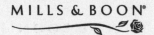

MILLS & BOON®

Makes
any time
special

Enjoy a romantic novel from
Mills & Boon®

Presents™ *Enchanted*™ *Temptation*

Historical Romance™ *Medical Romance*™

MILLS & BOON®

Next Month's Romance Titles

Each month you can choose from a wide variety of romance novels from Mills & Boon®. Below are the new titles to look out for next month from the Presents...™ and Enchanted™ series.

Presents...™

A CONVENIENT BRIDEGROOM	Helen Bianchin
IRRESISTIBLE TEMPTATION	Sara Craven
THE BAD GIRL BRIDE	Jennifer Drew
MISTRESS FOR A NIGHT	Diana Hamilton
A TREACHEROUS SEDUCTION	Penny Jordan
ACCIDENTAL BABY	Kim Lawrence
THE BABY GAMBIT	Anne Mather
A MAN TO MARRY	Carole Mortimer

Enchanted™

KIDS INCLUDED!	Caroline Anderson
PARENTS WANTED!	Ruth Jean Dale
MAKING MR RIGHT	Val Daniels
A VERY PRIVATE MAN	Jane Donnelly
LAST-MINUTE BRIDEGROOM	Linda Miles
DR. DAD	Julianna Morris
DISCOVERING DAISY	Betty Neels
UNDERCOVER BACHELOR	Rebecca Winters

On sale from 6th August 1999

H1 9907

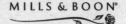

MILLS & BOON®

Medical Romance™

COMING NEXT MONTH from 6th August

ONE IN A MILLION by Margaret Barker
Bundles of Joy

Sister Tessa Grainger remembered Max Forster when he
arrived as consultant on her Obs and Gynae ward, for she'd
babysat when his daughter Francesca was small. But Max
wasn't the carefree man she'd known. Tessa wanted him to
laugh again and—maybe—even love again...

POLICE SURGEON by Abigail Gordon

Dr Marcus Owen was happy to be a GP and Police Surgeon,
until he found one of the practice partners was Caroline Croft,
the woman he'd once loved. Caroline was equally dismayed,
for she still loved Marcus! Brought back together by their
children, where did they go from here?

IZZIE'S CHOICE by Maggie Kingsley

Sister Isabella Clark came back to discover a new broom A&E
consultant, but being followed around by Ben Farrell ended
with her speaking her mind and Ben apologised! Since he liked
her "honesty", Izzie kept it up, but it wasn't until the hospital
fête that they realised they might have something more...

THE HUSBAND SHE NEEDS by Jennifer Taylor
A Country Practice #4

When District Nurse Abbie Fraser hears that Nick Delaney is
home, she isn't sure how she feels, for Nick is now in a
wheelchair. Surely she can make Nick see he has a future?
But at what cost to herself, when she realises she has never
stopped loving him?

*Available at most branches of WH Smith, Tesco, Asda,
Martins, Borders, Easons, Volume One/James Thin
and most good paperback bookshops*

MILLS & BOON®

Historical Romance™

Coming next month

LADY JANE'S PHYSICIAN
by Anne Ashley
A Regency Delight

Lady Jane Beresford visited her cousin, but her
enjoyment was marred by meeting Dr Thomas
Carrington. Tom's blunt attitudes irritated Jane out of
her own good manners! But he knew, if she didn't, that
an Earl's daughter was far above his touch…

UNTAMED HEART
by Georgina Devon
A Regency delight! ❦ *Book 1 of 3*

Lizabeth Johnstone was shocked by her primitive
reaction to Lord Alastair St. Simon. He should be every
woman's dream, but he wasn't *hers* for Alastair was
responsible for her younger's brother's death. Her
stubborn refusal to accept help left him with only one
alternative—they'd have to get married…

On sale from 6th August 1999

*Available at most branches of WH Smith, Tesco, Asda,
Martins, Borders, Easons, Volume One/James Thin
and most good paperback bookshops*

4 FREE
books and a surprise gift!

We would like to take this opportunity to thank you for reading this Mills & Boon® book by offering you the chance to take FOUR more specially selected titles from the Enchanted™ series absolutely FREE! We're also making this offer to introduce you to the benefits of the Reader Service™—

- ★ FREE home delivery
- ★ FREE gifts and competitions
- ★ FREE monthly Newsletter
- ★ Exclusive Reader Service discounts
- ★ Books available before they're in the shops

Accepting these FREE books and gift places you under no obligation to buy, you may cancel at any time, even after receiving your free shipment. Simply complete your details below and return the entire page to the address below. ***You don't even need a stamp!***

YES! Please send me 4 free Enchanted books and a surprise gift. I understand that unless you hear from me, I will receive 6 superb new titles every month for just £2.40 each, postage and packing free. I am under no obligation to purchase any books and may cancel my subscription at any time. The free books and gift will be mine to keep in any case.

N9EA

Ms/Mrs/Miss/Mr ....Initials........................
BLOCK CAPITALS PLEASE

Surname ....

Address ....

....

....Postcode........................

Send this whole page to:
THE READER SERVICE, FREEPOST CN81, CROYDON, CR9 3WZ
(Eire readers please send coupon to: P.O. BOX 4546, DUBLIN 24.)